THE
SECRET
GIFT

THE SECRET GIFT

Copyright © 2021 by Bethany Atazadeh

For information contact :

https://www.bethanyatazadeh.com

Cover design by Stone Ridge Books

First Edition: September 2021
10 9 8 7 6 5 4 3 2 1

THE SECRET GIFT

STOLEN KINGDOM NOVELLA
A VILLAIN ORIGIN STORY

BETHANY ATAZADEH

 GRACE HOUSE PRESS

ALSO BY

BETHANY ATAZADEH

SIGN UP FOR MY AUTHOR NEWSLETTER

Want to be in the loop ? Sign up for my monthly newsletter and be the first to learn new releases, plus receive exclusive content for both readers and writers!

WWW.BETHANYATAZADEH.COM/CONTACT

CHAPTER 1

"LET'S HOPE YOU NEVER develop that garbage Gift your mother had," my father grumbled after his second cup of mead. He was getting an early start tonight. "That woman thought she could use me to hide her shifting? I'll tell you what, in the end, I used her Gift to my advantage far more than she ever—" the rest was too muffled to hear, but it was no doubt the same litany of complaints I'd heard every night since I could remember.

He tossed his empty drink in my direction.

I didn't bother to duck. The wooden cup

bounced harmlessly across the stone floor only halfway across the room, dribbling liquid onto the surface that was now covered in stains.

"Jezebel. Another," he mumbled, closing his eyes and burrowing deeper into his Lacklore-hide chair. He draped his arms over the bear-like paws, claws still sharp, and leaned back beneath the ox-like head where it was stuffed and set into the tall back of the chair.

Growing up, I used to whine that he could take care of himself. Without fail, he would point to his legs—those legs that started out like any other Jinni male, but transformed into the legs of a goat. Hoofs and all. A permanent gift from my mother. Or, in this case, a curse.

"Yes, father." I lifted my chin and obeyed, bringing him a third full cup, setting it on the table beside him. My hand shook slightly. Straining against the desire to slam it down or scream at him, I kept my face serene, not revealing any hint of my feelings.

Sometimes I secretly wondered how my mother had stopped at the legs alone.

Our home was small. Only a few steps to get back to the sink, where I continued to slowly do the dishes. If I looked too idle, it'd encourage him to focus his bitter diatribe on me.

I stared out the kitchen window, past the faded blue curtains, at the street below where my few friends gathered. Asher waved when he saw me, but I couldn't wave back without giving myself away. Pressing my lips together in a pained smile, though he was too far below to see, I wished I was with them.

Other Jinn my age had mentors after their discipline years ended. As their Gifts manifested between the ages of fifteen to twenty-two, someone with similar Gifts would take them on and train them in how to use them. How to be a lethal weapon or a benefactor or anything in-between.

I was only seventeen, so some would say I still had time.

My secret Gift was still fairly new. It'd manifested a few short months ago, after I'd finished my discipline years. Thankfully, no one else was aware. And I, for the most part, was too terrified to use it.

Still, I'd never have a mentor because no one could know my true Gifts. My mother had made that clear.

Just five years old when she'd left, I'd gripped her short skirts and wrapped myself around her tall sandaled legs. "Please don't leave, mama."

"I have to, darling," she'd said, ruthlessly prying me off of her before retying the laces and strapping on her ornamental breastplate. "When you have Gifts like mine, that's all anyone can see. The royal family fears this Gift and wants to take control of my abilities, as your father did." She stood. "I'm not going to let them."

"But papa loves you," I'd cried.

"He loves my Gift," she'd snapped, bending down again to face me. "And I plan to break him of that." Her grip on my shoulders hurt as she shook me slightly. "Always remember this: don't share your Gifts with anyone, Jezebel. People will use them and use you. Better to keep them for yourself." She'd stood, brushing off her hands as if brushing me off for the final time. "If I could go back in time, I'd keep mine a secret. Then we would see who truly loved me."

If she would've known that I'd develop the same Gift as her years later, would she have stayed? Or better yet, would she have taken me with her? I still didn't know the answer to that, but I'd never forgotten those words. Part of me wanted to believe she was wrong. The burning question came back as it always did: if I showed my true self to someone, would it change how they saw me? Would they still love me?

My father certainly wouldn't. He hadn't been the same since she'd left.

"Your mother's Gift was as useless as her," he said now, sloshing his drink as he lifted himself out of the chair. He set the cup down and made his way to the bed on the far side of the room, falling into it. He'd moved it out of his bedroom to eliminate unnecessary steps.

That was my cue to go to my own room for the night, though it wasn't even dark out. Better to let him sleep it off than to make noise and risk waking him.

I dried my hands quickly, dimming the flickering ceiling lamp and pulling my door closed, when he muttered, "She was ugly besides."

Despite myself, I paused and looked back at him.

His cold eyes were on me, clear for once, aware of his cruelty. "You look just like her, Jezzie."

My hands twitched, wanting to touch my long, black hair and my pale face. Lips too small and thin. Brows too thick. Nose too long. I knew it all by heart.

Instead, I let the door to my room close softly,

refusing to give him the satisfaction. Though he didn't realize it, I could easily change all of that. And someday, I would. Someday, I promised myself I'd get away from him and find a place where I could be my true self. And I would never let anyone call me that name again.

The minutes passed slowly as I paced my tiny room, from one side of the small bed to the other, past my few possessions inside the dresser and the bare walls with peeling gray paint. Outside, the sun began to set.

Only when my father's heavy snores pierced the air did I finally steal toward my window and crack it open.

Our cramped living quarters were located on the third floor of the acropolis that surrounded the capital. Hundreds of Jinn lived in the little apartments above, below, and to the sides, as well as roamed the streets at any given time of day, so this was always a fear-inducing moment. It was far too high to jump, and the spells surrounding the acropolis prevented Jinn from traveling to the ground in a flash. Since there was no way I'd risk sneaking past my father, that left me with only one option.

I shifted as quickly as possible into a green lizard the size of my palm, glancing over my shoulder the whole time until it became green and scaly, along with my clothes, and basically ceased to exist. This form would be permanent until I chose to shift again.

Then, with those helpful sticky footpads, I crawled up the wall, out the window, and down the tall columns to my hidden corner near the acropolis' main entrance. In the dark space where no one could see, I shifted back to myself—short white dress, sandals, gold arm bands, and all.

Being forced to keep my Gift to myself meant I didn't always know exactly *how* it worked the way it did, but as far as I could tell, it was like molding clay and reshaping it into something new. I had to do it a little bit at a time, but as I got used to sculpting certain things, they came to me quicker. Such as returning to myself; that always snapped back into place.

All four of my friends stood in the shade of the acropolis, lounging by one of the passways. They all had ebony hair and pale, almost translucent skin with a hint of blue veins beneath like all Jinn, but that was where the similarities ended.

"Bel," Asher called softly, his deep-red eyes flashing in excitement as I strode up to them. "We were starting to wonder if you were coming!"

I warmed to him and the nickname as always, to the whole different person I became with them, though I still kept my shifting a secret.

"You know I have to wait for old donkey-legs to fall asleep," I retorted, but I let the corner of my mouth tip up a bit. Summer heat radiated off the dark-stone street, even now after the sun had set. "What're we doing tonight?"

Besides Asher, our group was made up of three other adolescent Jinn: tiny Phillipa, whose strongest Gift let her sense when fruit was ripe, obnoxious Simon, whose main Gift allowed him to put himself and others to sleep, and the ill-tempered Miriam who—like Asher—couldn't claim a single Gift. Not even the most common Gift of Traveling. Which meant I fit in with them perfectly. As far as they knew, traveling was my only Gift, and only short distances.

Other Jinn our age looked down on us; often they wouldn't even acknowledge our presence, as was evidenced by a small group of former friends walking past right now who pretended we weren't there. Our own parents saw us as a disappointment. Since we weren't strong enough to be considered for the Jinni Guard, and most of us couldn't even acquire a basic mentor, we were for the most part left to ourselves. Until eventually, one by one, we'd be forced to take on some kind of menial labor.

"We can't talk here," Asher whispered, which immediately made me perk up. Secrets were Jinni bread and butter. It must be an especially good secret to worry that another Gifted one might overhear. "Take us to the usual place," Asher commanded, holding out a hand.

Times like this, when his insecurities about being Gift-less made him sharp, I oddly liked him more. To be seen as powerless—well, I knew the feeling better than he realized.

So, I simply took his hand and traveled with him to the edge of the main island where the others had already landed.

When we glanced back at the enormous capital city of Resh we'd left behind, it looked like a miniature toy town in the distance, with the acropolis stretching protectively all around it. The castle rose above everything else in the center, glowing white in the moonlight.

Here at the edge of the island, clouds drifted past, close enough to reach out and touch. Somewhere far below, too distant to see from our elevation, was the human world. And there to the right, floating in and out of clouds, was Urim, one of the smaller Jinni islands. It was close enough that many Jinn could travel the distance between these particular islands without the use of the bridges.

Not the five of us, of course… but some.

Asher pulled his hand away as soon as we landed, and I tried not to let my disappointment show. He turned to the others who stood in a half-circle. Miriam was next to Simon, since he'd brought her. Her wrinkled forehead and crossed arms said she felt the same as Asher about their lack of abilities. Simon might've brought Phillipa too, I couldn't tell; though she could travel on her own, she preferred to stick with one of us and fade into the background of our little group.

After a quick glance around, to where tall grasses swayed in the bright moonlight on one side and the island dropped off on the other, I whispered, "You have to tell us! I can't stand the suspense!"

Asher's pinched lips relaxed into a smile. Knowledge was a kind of power, after all. He waved for us to follow him into the trees. "Remember our discipline years, when they taught us what a *Daleth* was?"

"A portal to the human world," Miriam snapped, though her expertise didn't seem to make her feel better. She hated being out in nature. "What of it?"

"I found one."

Simon immediately traveled in front of Asher to halt him in his tracks, though he'd only been two steps away. He liked to show off the meager skills he did have. "You're making that up."

"You wish," Asher said with a grin, hitting Simon's decorative silver breastplate as he stepped around him.

"Those don't pop up one day out of nowhere," Miriam said, swatting at bugs as she followed. "How would no one have found it before? I don't think it's really a portal at all, you're just trying to trick us."

"You'll see." Asher didn't stop, grinning over his shoulder. "This one is nearly impossible to stumble onto. If I hadn't tried to pick a specific herb right between two trees, I'd have missed it myself."

The details made me start to believe him. My heartbeat sped up. We could use information like that as a way to curry favor with the royal family—maybe find a better profession at the castle than what we were destined for. Better yet, being introduced to such powerful Jinn could help me finally get away from my father completely.

Maybe it'd even produce an opportunity to meet

the handsome Prince Shem. I glanced over at Miriam and Phillipa, wondering if they were thinking the same thing.

The royals were always looking for Daleths. For whatever reason, they liked to have control over them. Probably because an unguarded portal was asking for trouble when it came to adolescent Jinn like us.

At the smirk on Asher's face, I sighed.

He'd chosen the trouble.

Leading us away from the edge of the island, on a curving path through the grass and the trees, he couldn't stop talking. "I found it when I was looking for some star anise." His cheeks blushed slightly blue. Since his natural-born Gifts were non-existent, he'd been determined to learn Jinni spells and enchantments instead. Though we all knew this, he changed the subject quickly. "Besides the Jinni Guard, no one we know has ever visited the human world."

"Except for Master Yeshiva," Miriam reminded him. All of our thoughts turned to the teacher we'd had briefly during our discipline years, right around the time we'd all met. He'd been banished to the human world for breaking one of the Three Unbreakable Laws: *Never use a Gift to deceive, never use a Gift to steal, and never use a Gift to harm another.* To this day, we still didn't know which one he'd broken.

"Well, we don't know anyone personally who's ever come *back*," Asher modified. "We're going to be the first! We'll see this human world with our own eyes, instead of hearing dull bedtime stories about it. Maybe we'll even have a little fun with the humans themselves."

He and Simon chuckled as each tried to hit the other's breastplate first, making the showy armor clang loudly when Simon succeeded.

I shuddered at the thought of interacting with humans, exchanging tight-lipped glances with Miriam and Phillipa.

Humans were said to be slimy to the touch and terribly unsanitary. Not to mention their intelligence level was about the same as one of our mutton grazers. You couldn't approach them in groups or you'd be more likely to be attacked than greeted.

We had a few humans living in the capital city of Resh, but it was rare, and usually only for a short time before someone with the Gift of Memories made them forget. They were usually employed by Jinn who thought they had a special talent or ability they needed. I couldn't fathom it. What could a human do that a Jinni couldn't?

Though the dangers of the human world didn't appeal to me, I trailed along behind them anyway.

Asher drew up next to a seemingly empty space between two trees that gently arched toward each other. Other than that, there was nothing to indicate they were anything special. Gesturing to the bark on one, where some scratches created a poorly carved circle, he said, "I marked it so we can find it whenever we want."

"But do we *really* want to go to the human world?" I finally spoke up, arching a brow at him.

"Everyone knows they're inferior," Miriam agreed, though coming from her it didn't mean much. "I hardly see the point."

Asher ignored her and stepped through the space between the trees. He disappeared.

"The *point*—" Simon mocked her "—is to have a little fun. But if you're as scared as an actual human and want to stay behind, then we'll see you when we get back." With that, he followed Asher.

Unlike traveling, where the whole body vanished at once, the daleth seemed to almost eat his body, swallowing it in pieces.

Miriam shook her head at the empty space, while

Phillipa glanced between us, and I rolled my eyes.

When Asher stuck his head back through unexpectedly, I was closest, and I couldn't help myself—I squeaked.

He roared with laughter. Miriam shoved his head back through and followed, no doubt anxious to prove herself. Giving me a small shrug, Phillipa stepped through next.

Once again, I brought up the rear.

Throwing my head back, I took a deep breath, then pressed through the invisible portal to the human world. The tingle of magic on my skin as I passed through made me shiver.

In the dark, it surprised me how similar it appeared to home. Though the moon above was naturally smaller from this lower vantage point, the rest of the landscape wasn't terrible. Wildflowers grew along the edge of the woods. A town on the hill ahead shone like a cheerful lamp, lights flickering in windows and laughter flooding out all the way to where we stood in the clearing.

Asher was already moving.

From the dark edges of the forest, we were still invisible to the humans, but there were at least a dozen of them ahead, hurrying in different directions like little ants on a mission.

"Wait for us," I called softly, rushing to take his elbow and pressure him into waiting for the rest of us. Though I'd never made my feelings for him known, I liked to think I held *some* sway over him. He did slow a bit, even if he refused to stop altogether. I tugged harder to get his attention. "What exactly are you hoping to accomplish here?"

With a glance back at the others, he leaned in to whisper, "I'd like to talk to one."

I frowned. *A human? Why?* Glancing up at his feverishly bright eyes, I could tell there'd be no arguing with him.

Still I tried. "We won't blend in." I waved toward Miriam, Phillipa, and myself with our short skirts and sandals that laced all the way up our bare calves, then at the village ahead. "The human women dress much more conservatively than the Jinn."

Phillipa and Miriam nodded sagely, attempting to hide their relief as they slowed to a stop.

"That's fair. You can wait here, if you'd like," Asher said over his shoulder, not pausing in his stride. I stuffed down my disappointment yet again. He could be stubborn when he was focused on something.

"We should probably make a plan first," Simon

tried, when I glanced over at him in desperation.

Finally, Asher stopped pressing forward. Turning to face us, he waved his hands wide. "Why must you all make everything so difficult? We're just going to talk to them."

"But what about the Unbreakable Laws?" Phillipa asked in her high, reedy voice.

"You think I somehow forgot about them?" Asher snapped, fists clenched at his sides. "We're not going to use our Gifts to steal from anyone, deceive anyone, or harm anyone, because none of us has *any real Gifts* in the first place."

The reminder dulled the pulsing excitement in the air for a moment. Technically, we all had more Gifts than him except for Miriam, but he was sensitive to that, so none of us mentioned it.

I pondered the advantages of the human world as I searched their faces. What if I didn't even worry about talking to a human at all, but instead found a safe place to finally explore my Gift outside of the tiny boundaries of my bedroom at night? I flexed my fingers tentatively. What if I could test my limits? See what else I could do? The others never needed to know. The freedom that had always been out of my reach tempted me like a rare dessert.

"Fine," I pulled away from the uneven circle toward the town. "We'll all talk to a human. Meet back here by midnight."

"Wait, Bel," Asher hissed as he caught up to me. "I, uh, I kind of thought we'd all talk to a human together."

"We can't," I said, ignoring the other's nods and my own little thrill at him admitting he wanted me there—even if he did lump the others in too. "If we all show up in one place, it'll be far too suspicious."

Not to mention it'd ruin my half-formed plans. "We must each go alone. Avoid any crowds, only talk to a human if they're on their own, and make sure you have an escape route if it goes poorly. Understand?"

"Who put you in charge?" Miriam muttered, but she didn't seem to expect an answer, and I didn't bother to give one. It felt good to lead for once.

CHAPTER 2

AT THE EDGE OF the town, our collective nerves made us huddle together behind a big stone wall outside a ring of lantern light. "Who's going first?" I asked, trying to sound nonchalant.

"My eyes are going to stand out too much," Asher complained, blinking his red eyes owlishly at the rest of us.

"You always do this." I crossed my arms, irritated that his worries made me question my own decisions. *Is it foolish to try this?* "You convince us to do something and then back out last minute."

As expected, this made him dig in his heels. "I didn't say I wasn't going. I'll have to make sure they don't see my eyes, that's all." Training on humans was part of all Jinni discipline years: we all had a basic understanding of their race, how to interact with them if we were ever allowed to venture into their world, and how incredibly little they knew about our own culture. Though they had many tall tales from occasional rare sightings of a reckless Jinni or two, the current royal family had made it a precedent over the last couple centuries to erase any memories of our more distinct differences. Such as our wide variety of eye colors.

My own eyes, though a paler blue than any normal human color, would be far less revealing.

"We all have a handicap we have to deal with," I reminded him, pointing to my bare, sandaled legs. Those would stand out just as much in this town as his eyes. Maybe more, since they'd be much harder to hide.

Without another word, I strode past him into the perimeter of the town.

Alone.

Keeping to the shadows, I didn't glance back until I'd walked past a dozen buildings. At that point, as far as I could tell, everyone had gone their own way. I had until midnight for my little experiment.

Anticipation made me walk faster, until I was practically running, dodging down one dark alley after the next.

The first creature I stumbled upon in the dark shadows of a private alleyway was not a human, but a dog. It ignored me, rummaging through some garbage. No other living soul was nearby to see.

Without thinking twice, I shifted into the same form. It was a breed we didn't have in Jinn, but the composition of the creature was the same: four legs on the ground, lengthier spine, and my nose extended further from my face as my jaws grew sharp canines. Once I'd seen it, it wasn't too difficult to replicate. The whole transformation took only a few minutes.

Letting out a cheerful bark at the real dog, I silently laughed as it backed up with hackles raised. I took off, racing along the packed dirt between homes at full speed, enjoying the wind in my fur.

I dug in deeper, taking one alleyway after another. Back home, I'd only dared the smallest of creatures, ones that a Jinni wouldn't look twice at. I reveled in this new form.

The downside of this creature, however, was the

sense of smell. Some of these alleyways were full of human filth that overpowered my new nose.

Tentatively, I played with my Gift, feeling my way through something that I should have been taught, until I finally discovered how to block the nasal passage. Perfect.

Halfway down one alleyway, I drew up short, panting. There was a human boy at the other end. Young. No more than four or five years old.

This would be a much more difficult stretch of my abilities and would probably use up most of my strength.

I exulted in the challenge.

Shaping my fur into skin as I reformed my endoskeleton within, I left the fine details of the little boy's face for last, adding a smattering of freckles under newly brown eyes and overly-long straw colored hair.

His eyes grew large as saucers as I transformed, but he didn't make a sound.

I took a testing step toward him, into the small ring of lamplight by the door.

The little boy's lower lip began to tremble.

I attempted to copy him.

He stumbled back against the wall of the home and let out a wail that pierced the night.

The door of the house flung open, bathing me in light. "Naseem," the woman cried, sweeping me up in her arms where I stood stunned.

My whole body tensed.

A human was touching me.

I wanted to make the same noises the other child had at the awful sensation.

The real Naseem had cut off his cries when the door opened and now met my gaze with shocked eyes as his mother whirled back inside, completely unaware, and shut the door between us.

"My little escape artist," the woman clucked as she moved toward the stove, bouncing me on her hip in a way that made my head hurt. I tried amidst the jiggling to get a sense of the small human home. There were two other children playing a game on one of the beds, and a stove took up the nearest wall. "Want to help me clean up dinner?" she asked, turning her face toward mine.

I panicked. Not only was I in the clutches of an awful human, but she was about to discover the truth any moment because I couldn't answer her—the human child had never spoken! Even if I'd had practice in shifting my own vocal cords to match someone else's, I had nothing to match!

"What's wrong, Naseem?" The woman's forehead wrinkled, and she stopped the horrible bouncing to focus all her attention on me.

Not knowing what else to do, I burrowed my face in her scratchy blouse and hid.

A hand patted my head, comforting. Through my fear, I noticed it wasn't slimy like the stories said at all; her skin was warm and dry, like my own, though a bit rougher. That knowledge didn't make the danger any less though.

"Don't worry, love," she said, going back to that unbearable bouncing. "Your baba will be home soon."

What's a baba? I wondered, but I didn't dare lift my head without risking more questions. This had been a huge mistake. I never should've agreed to come. *What if I don't make it home?* The humans would discover me and cook me in a stew. Or trap me in a cage to entertain them. Already the woman's arms had begun to feel like steel bars.

When she set me on a bed, I didn't hesitate to crawl under the itchy blanket and close my eyes, refusing to open them until her footsteps shuffled back toward the stove.

Barely a full minute had passed for me to begin forming a plan, before the wooden door swung open and a human man stepped inside, holding the *real* Naseem. "Look who I found outside again," he said, chuckling.

I flung the blanket over my head and shifted into the smallest creature I could think of, littler than anything I'd ever attempted before—a tiny flea.

If I hadn't already been smaller than usual, it wouldn't have worked, but by the time the woman stepped up to the bed and flung back the covers, I'd burrowed into the thin straw mattress and was already halfway to the other side.

"What kind of Jinni magic—" the wife grumbled to her husband, but I'd stopped listening.

Instead, I crawled out of the mattress along a thin piece of a straw into the darkness beneath the bed and shifted into my most familiar shape: the green lizard.

All that mattered right now was escape.

Crawling painstakingly beneath the furniture along the edges of the room, I managed to remain unseen all the way to the door, where I shifted back into a flea, and slipped through a crack at the base.

Outside in the dark, I wanted to sob, but my flea form wasn't capable.

All this shifting had left me beyond exhausted.

Starving.

I struggled to return to my own form. After so many shifts in such a short span of time, it took far longer than normal.

As long minutes passed, I ached and stretched and shuddered until finally I could wipe a tear from my own cheek.

Then, I forced myself to stop crying.

Years with my father had taught me to keep my emotions in check until it was safe, though I'd never been tested like this before.

Dragging myself to my sandaled feet, I nearly broke down again at the thought of trying to cross the entire town without discovery. I just wanted to go home. To never see or think of a human again.

So many vast changes in a row and at such speed had sapped my strength to the point that my muscles trembled and left me famished. I needed food and rest. As soon as possible.

Traveling was out of the question. So was changing into the dog form or any other. I could hardly think past my hunger.

What an awful, awful night.

I needed time to regain my strength. Time I didn't have.

I can't lean against the wall of this house all

night, waiting to be caught.

I needed a simple shift. Something manageable.

There was one thing I'd never tried before.

In a normal transition my clothes always shifted with me, which meant I'd never changed the clothing alone. I'd never needed to.

Since this part of my Gift had always come naturally to me, I decided to try it on its own now.

Lengthening my short skirts until they reached my ankles, like the ones the human mother had worn, turned out to be as easy as touching the fabric and picturing it longer. It took almost no effort, and sapped almost no strength.

I sagged back against the wall when I tried to turn my pale blue eyes into brown like hers, though. Once I managed it, no further shifting was needed to blend in.

Slipping out into the quiet streets like this, I finally allowed myself to draw a full breath.

There was at least an hour until midnight, maybe more.

I needed rest, and if possible, something to eat.

Hoping to regain my strength as soon as possible, I walked slowly, taking my time. An apple pie sat cooling in a window and I stole it without pausing, not even feeling guilty since it was made by one of those vile humans.

I ate it in crumbly bites with my fingers as I walked.

Still ravenous, I used the tiny bit of energy the food gave me to travel inside a nearby home, hoping the lack of light under the door meant they were asleep. Shuffling through their kitchen, I snacked on anything and everything I could get my hands on, no matter how unfamiliar it tasted. Then, curling up in a dark corner in the pantry, I closed my eyes, leaned my head back against the wall, and rested.

Shifting finally started to feel within reach again, a little bit at a time, as the minutes passed. It was almost like when a leg fell asleep, and then it would tingle as it woke up and make itself known again.

Satisfied, I traveled back into the dark streets, noting the time—close to midnight now—and continued on.

Most of my anxiety had melted away by the time the outer wall of the village came into sight.

I laughed softly, feeling foolish now.

I hadn't been in any real danger.

The humans would never know I'd been there. By the time the boy was old enough to explain, he'd think he'd imagined it. And now, I was practically home.

Another few houses, and I would stop in the shadows to change my dress and eyes back to normal.

Part of me wished I would've enjoyed my time here a bit more.

"Hello, sweetheart," a male voice said.

The corner of my mouth twisted upward. It was as if someone had granted my wish. If I'd still been tired, I would have simply traveled away, but my playful mood was back in full force.

I stood in a circle of lamplight, and the man was somewhere behind me. Taking advantage of this, I quickly grew facial hair, forming an entire beard like the so-called "Baba" had worn earlier. It was detailed work, but excitement spurred me on, making me add other details like wrinkled, old skin and bags under my eyes. A few tucks and tweaks to my body, and by the time I turned to face the voice, I was an old man wearing a slightly odd robe instead of a dress.

The leer on the drunken man's face froze.

It was an effort not to burst out laughing. Staying in character, I raised my now bushy gray brows and made a rude gesture, before I turned back around and kept walking. Only then did I allow a smirk to reach my face.

The only damper in my fun was that I still didn't know how to shift my voice.

As I listened to the disgusting man shuffle off, I played with my vocal chords, stretching them this way, then that. Certain changes lowered my voice until it was almost manly, while other changes made it high and childish—but could I ever learn to imitate a specific voice, like the little boy from earlier? Truly replace someone? Maybe I could learn to imitate someone like my father, who's voice I knew all too well, but that would take practice and experimenting on my own to know for sure.

I'd discovered my Gift months ago, and yet, I still knew so little.

Scowling at the reminder that I was weak without a teacher, I started walking again and forced a faster shift than normal, pushing myself. I returned to my true form—short dress, sandals, and long, dark hair grazing my bare arms and back—without pausing in my stride.

A gasp came from the shadows on my left.

The usual instinct to flee surged through me.

I swung around.

Too late.

Asher stood in the dark alley between homes, where he must've been waiting for the others to return. Maybe he'd never left this spot. My fingers curled into helpless fists. How much had he seen?

"Haven't you been hiding a valuable little secret?" he whispered, slowly grinning. "Wait until the others find out about this."

"What're you talking about?" I scoffed, hiding my panic. "Are you feeling ill? I've been here nearly ten minutes now, and you've been babbling about all the humans you saw." I reached out as if to feel his brow for a fever.

He frowned, pulling back and shaking his head. "Nice try. I saw all of it. First, you grew a beard for that creep and changed your voice, then you made all of it disappear just now in a breath." Every word made my heart sink. "You're a shape-shifter!"

For a beat, we simply stared at each other.

What tack should I take now?

I'd always liked Asher, but liking and trusting were very different things.

"It's okay," he said softly, as if he could sense my uncertainty. "If you don't want me to tell anyone, I won't. You can trust me, Bel."

It was the nickname that made my mask slip. I

stepped closer and hissed, "You have to swear to keep it a secret."

Though he swallowed hard, he didn't step back. That alone gave me hope. "I promise."

Another long silence passed between us, heavy with unasked questions.

"So, why *is* it a secret?" he blurted, curiosity making him lean forward. "You have a Gift that's actually *worth* something. Sure, it's considered a bit dangerous by some, but that's only because it's so rare. You could be working with a mentor right now—"

"It just is," I bit out. If only my secret Gift could've been shifting memories instead of physical shapes.

Before he could ask more, Simon materialized a few paces down the road, right under a street lamp, not the slightest bit concerned about humans seeing his Gift.

I supposed after what Asher had seen me do, I couldn't really judge him.

"You should've been there!" Simon chortled, completely unaware of the tension between Asher and I as he jogged over and joined us in the dark alley. "I put a whole tavern to sleep! It was crazy! I can't believe my mentor won't let me try stuff like this back home. I could do so much more than they think!"

The mention of a mentor made Asher swing back to face me, and I couldn't break free of his gaze.

"Where is everyone?" At the other end of the street, Miriam's voice drifted toward us. "This isn't funny," she whined, getting louder as she let her nerves make her forget the humans all around. "If you all thought you could travel home and leave me here, I'm going to mix up a curse so strong you won't be able to sit for a year."

Simon leaned out, not noticing the intensity of our stare. "Oh, get over yourself, Miriam. You couldn't curse a pinky toe if you tried."

His jab made me shake my head in annoyance, finally breaking the spell. "Don't be so sure of that," I said to Simon, standing up for sensitive Miriam. "You're practically begging to be her first true curse."

Once I'd looked away from Asher, I couldn't seem to meet his eyes again.

What must he think of me now? Any hope that he might return my feelings someday had been crushed.

Stepping out into the street, I forced my hands to

stay at my sides and my feet to take casual strides, though the light made me feel exposed. Made me want to run. "Let's go home," I said to all of them as I passed Miriam, who fell into step behind me.

We found Phillipa leaning against a tree outside the short stone wall where we'd first entered the town, arms crossed, shoulders slumped. She ignored all of us as we drew closer, though we weren't making any effort to be quiet.

"What happened to you?" Simon asked, nudging her shoulder less roughly than usual.

"Nothing," she muttered. "I don't want to talk about it."

A piece of her dress was ripped at the shoulder. Though she didn't have the best life at home, I could've sworn it hadn't been that way when we'd first arrived. I waited until the others moved toward the portal before I took her arm and tucked it under mine, bending to her ear to ask softly, "Did a human hurt you?"

"Nothing serious," she murmured back, staring aimlessly ahead. "I traveled away before…" She didn't finish whatever she'd been planning to say.

Despicable humans. I gritted my teeth, feeling a fury so strong it made me shake. "We should make him pay."

Phillipa's voice shook. "I just want to go home."

I was so sick of bullies. My father was the worst of them. But they were everywhere. People—whether Jinn or human—couldn't help but prey on others; it was in our nature. And humans were without a doubt the lowest scum.

"Are you coming?" Asher called from ahead, standing beside the trunk of the tree that marked our passage home. His eyes were on me. When I met them, he held my gaze until I broke it again.

It was good he'd tied a bit of red string to mark the portal on the human world side, because the daleth itself was invisible. The trees stood so close together that to pass through and return home, we had to each take turns, sucking in our breath and squeezing past the rough bark to make it to the other side.

"Go ahead," I told Phillipa, wanting for some reason to go last. As her foot disappeared, I stared at the dark patch of foliage beyond. A soft wind made the leaves rustle all around me and an owl hooted somewhere off in the darkness. From here, the town we'd visited transformed into a twinkle of lights in the distance.

What was I going to do about Asher? I wanted

to trust him, but I didn't know if I could.

While I stood frozen, worrying over it, his head popped back through the daleth and smiled at me.

Startled yet again, I reared back and shot him a glare.

"I haven't said a word to the others," he said, as if he knew I needed to hear it. "We can talk about it more tomorrow, but don't worry. I won't tell anyone." Winking, he joked, "Yet."

At least, I hoped he was joking.

CHAPTER 3

MEET ME BY THE *daleth*, his note had said. He didn't sign it, but he didn't need to, because only Asher slipped notes under the door when my father was out.

Normally, I loved this. I kept a jar of his previous notes beneath my bed—even if all they ever said were things like, *Boaz got a new Gift. Such a braggart.* Or, *See if you can get me some Tradandar at the market for my new spell.*

Today though, anxiety chased me around the small apartment no matter how fast I cooked and cleaned. I managed to finish my chores and slip out before my father ever came home.

By the time I reached the daleth in the last bits of golden light before the sun set, Asher had clearly been waiting a while. "I brought you honey cakes," he said as I strode up the hill toward him. "But I ate them all." Crumbs dusted his upper lip, stuck amidst the slight dark fuzz growing there.

I turned away to look at the view and smiled a little despite myself. Shading my eyes, I waited for him to lead this conversation.

From this height, the whole capital city of Resh stretched out below, seemingly calm from a distance. The river Mem lazily split the city in two, winding off to the north. Up close, it would be a roaring giant, but from here it was as thin as a string.

"I just wondered," he finally said, when I didn't turn around or speak. "You know, if you were going to tell me at some point… why you kept your Gift a secret?" He stepped in front of me, so that I couldn't help but look at him. His brows lifted suspiciously. "Do you have *other* secret Gifts?"

I laughed. Shaking my head at him, I moved to sit on the grassy hill. "What a question," I answered in the usual Jinni way of not answering at all, giving him half a smile. This would most likely make him think I did indeed have other Gifts.

I did not. At least, none that had revealed themselves yet. But just like the others, I wished I did. Didn't all Jinn? Our abilities were everything: power, wealth, stability…

It might still be possible, to have a latent Gift, not yet discovered. It happened sometimes.

At the very least, Asher wasn't the only one attempting to learn spells and enchantments in his free time, though unlike him, I didn't advertise the fact.

Accepting my non-answer, he simply shrugged and sat beside me, switching to a different question. "What exactly can you shift into? Can you look like other Jinn?" There was a hint of fear beneath his bravado. A slight tremor in his voice that he tried to hide with a laugh. "Can you become *me*?"

Instead of the landscape below, I saw the freckled face of the little boy from the human world. I shivered, knowing the answer, even without a mentor. I could shift into anyone, with enough time, energy, and rest.

Part of me wanted to trust Asher, to open up about everything… Would he try to control me like my parents had each other? Like everyone else I'd known? Or could he be trusted?

"I don't know," I lied, finally. "I'm not sure if I'm that skilled."

"Why don't you work with a mentor and find out?" he asked, letting his arms hang over his knees as he played with a long strand of grass.

Back to that question. "I can't." My voice came out almost in a whisper.

This time, he was the one who waited patiently.

I ran a hand through the long grasses too. Sighing, I pulled my arms in to hug my knees. "People will want to exploit you," I quoted my mother the day she'd left us. "It's better when you don't give them something to use." Out of the corner of my eye, I tried to read his reaction as he swung around to stare at me.

"That's ridiculous," he scoffed. "Why do you think we all hang out together? It's not like any of us have any valuable Gifts—" he caught himself, glancing at me "—not that we were aware of, at least. And we still hang out with each other."

That was true.

Hesitating, I considered the possibilities. One huge secret was already out, what would another hurt? Maybe it'd be a relief? I made myself turn to him and be far more honest than usual. "We weren't spending time with each other for our abilities. But, maybe you did want *something*?" I leaned in closer, letting my eyes drift to his lips and then slowly back up to his red eyes, making myself as clear as I could without spelling it out.

He laughed. "So what if I did? Or do?" he added, winking. I didn't dare move, staying slightly too close, feeling his breath on my face as he continued. "That doesn't mean I'm 'exploiting' you. Unless, of course, you aren't interested?"

I swallowed, heartbeat speeding up. He'd put me on the spot now.

I should pull back. That'd be easier. "That's not it…" I said instead. I planned to add more, but couldn't seem to find any other words.

It seemed to be enough.

He leaned in, closing the rest of the gap. His lips brushed mine softly. "I don't want to take advantage of you," he said huskily against my mouth. "If anything, I want *you* to take advantage of *me*."

I felt his grin more than saw it, but was too caught up in the kiss to answer.

He took the hint and stopped talking.

This wasn't my first kiss, but it was the first that meant something. My whole body felt shimmery and light, as if I could turn into a butterfly just by sensation alone.

Was this what my mother meant when she said people used you? Maybe it was worth the risk…

I kissed him back, tucking the thought away to ponder more later.

Pulling away unexpectedly, Asher whispered, "Show me what you can do?"

Eyes half-closed, it took me a moment to orient myself and remember what he was talking about. I drew a breath to divert him again, then paused. The temptation to reveal my Gift to someone after hiding for so long tugged at me. Maybe just once? After all, he'd already seen it, so it wasn't really anything new.

"Not here," I found myself saying. No way I was going to risk being discovered by another Jinn passing by. Standing, I headed for the daleth, anxiety and excitement warring within me as I hurried toward it.

A glance over my shoulder assured me he followed, practically on my heels, before I slipped through the portal into the human world for the second time in as many days.

Again, it struck me how the other side was deceptively the same as ours. Green grass, tall trees, blue skies, and a gentle breeze, although the sun peeking through the clouds was smaller down here. During the day, we might not have ever discovered the town, without the lights drawing us toward it.

This time, we instinctively moved through the trees in the opposite direction, putting distance between us and the foreign creatures. Not that the humans could do much to us. But keeping secrets was in our blood.

"What do you want me to be?" I asked over my shoulder as we went, inexplicably shy.

"You mean who?"

"No, I can be animals too."

He shook his head in disbelief. "No way. Bel, you know how unusual that is, don't you? I haven't met a full-blooded shape-shifter in... well, ever."

"My mom was full-blooded too," I whispered. Neither my father or I had ever told anyone that since before she disappeared. It was her secret. When asked about his legs, my father would always say he'd offended a powerful Jinni once and leave it at that.

Asher stopped in a small clearing, whirling to face me. "Wait, was she the one that changed him?"

The worry on his face made me lie without thinking. "No, of course not. She wouldn't break the

Unbreakable Laws like that."

He mimed wiping his brow in relief and smiled, then straightened suddenly. "If you both have the same Gift, did she at least teach you anything before she left?"

I shook my head. The disappointment when I thought of her stole my voice for a minute. "I—I've had to teach myself," I repeated, souring more each time he made me say so.

Biting his lip as if he could tell he'd harped on it long enough, he swung around to sit on a fallen log at the edge of the circle. "Show me your favorite shift?" He'd carefully made it a question.

Taking a deep breath, I nodded.

The lizard.

I stepped onto the log beside him, towering over him for a moment, which made him lean back at first, then lean forward in surprise as, a half-minute later, he found himself peering down at my small, green, four-legged shape. I flicked my tongue out at him to signal it was complete.

"Wow," he said on a breath. "I'd have never…" He shook his head, searching for words. "Can you go smaller?"

I dipped my leathery chin in a nod, and shrunk down to the flea I'd tried the previous night. Because it was familiar now, the change was not nearly as difficult. In fact, I could still change maybe two or even three times more before I began to tire. If my flea form could've smiled, I would have.

As it was, Asher had dropped his face until he was level with the trunk, trying to find me.

I gave a little hop.

"No way!" His response almost blew me away. Literally. "Can you… can you grow larger as well as smaller?"

I took my time, answering through shifting, forming first a large body, then thick, muscled bear-like legs with elongated claws, and the ox-like head of a Lacklore.

This was a creature I'd never attempted before; not only would it have been impossible to hide my Gift if I'd attempted it in the city, but I'd also never seen one alive in person, only a stuffed one in a museum plus the partial pelt on my father's chair.

As a result, shifting was far more difficult and time-consuming, as I tried to visualize the living version. I wished I'd brought a snack along; after a change this drastic I was going to be hungry.

When I finally blinked my huge black eyes at him, he just blinked back, stunned.

I studied the long length of the claws and the way they left deep gouges in the soft grass and dirt. Lifting one of those sharp claws, I wiggled it in a wave at Asher.

He instinctively jumped back. Blushing when he caught himself, he forced a hoarse laugh. "I don't know what to say. It's—You're—I just… I can't believe you've kept this a secret. Shift back so you can talk to me! Do you realize all the things you could do with this Gift?"

I took longer than I really needed to return to my Jinni form, partly to conserve my strength but also to give me time to think about what he meant.

One thing I hadn't shown him yet, which I'd barely even begun to experiment with, was touching up my face. As I shifted back to my usual form, I enhanced my dark lashes and the rosy tint of my lips and cheeks, deepening the blue in my eyes from a pale shallow pool to a deep, clear lake. As my sharpened teeth returned to their usual rounded state, I made them straighter and when I smiled at Asher, I paid close attention to see if he'd notice any of the minor changes.

He stood squinting at me with a small crease in his brows. "Why is it that I feel as if I'm seeing you differently? It's like I never truly saw you before?"

This time I did laugh. A light happiness settled over me. Instead of pointing out what I'd done, I just smiled at him.

I might keep the changes going forward, maybe even make a few other adjustments... as long as I didn't let my father see. They were easy enough to shift. So minor, in fact, that it took about as much effort as walking a step. And once I set them in place, they'd be as permanent as all my other changes, staying exactly this way until I made another change.

It occurred to me for the first time that perhaps I never needed to age. That I might live longer than most Jinn, maybe even... forever?

My eyes widened.

Forever was an incredibly long time. Long enough to escape my father for good. To leave bad memories behind. Maybe to become something—or someone—new?

Turning my back on Asher for a moment to savor this new revelation without letting him see, I walked to the middle of the clearing before I turned back to him.

Finally, I answered his question about what all I could do. "Probably more than I have imagined." Gesturing to my short day dress that ended above my knees, I touched the pale cream fabric to focus my ability, and it extended into an evening gown that brushed the soft, grassy floor.

This, I had learned out of necessity the night before. Now I took it a step further. Still clutching the soft fabric, I imagined a different color and before our eyes the cream turned into a deep teal as if it'd been doused in a dye.

"Does it have to be touching you?" Asher asked with wide, curious eyes as he stepped closer to get a better look. "Or does it remain changed even when you... take it off?" A blue blush rose in his pale cheeks, though he held my gaze.

"Are you trying to get me out of my dress?" I meant to sound flirtatious and confident, but the words came out breathy and girlish.

Before he could answer and make the situation more awkward, I dropped to the ground to sit, pulling the dress back to view my sandals, which were laced all the way from my ankle to my knee.

The wrap style was way too thick and out of fashion. With a touch to the tan laces to orient myself, I attempted to thin them into the elegance of the current style, changing them to a shimmery teal as well, to match my lavish gown.

Though it worked, I bit my lip as I unlaced one

of them slowly. Part of me wished Asher wasn't here. I didn't like to experiment when others were around. But now that he'd given me the idea, I had to know.

Untying the last lace, I slipped the sandal off.

Asher crouched down across from me.

I met his eyes briefly before I set it ceremoniously between us… and let go.

It reverted immediately to its true form.

Thick, old, tan laces.

Clenching my fists, I struggled to breathe calmly and not show Asher how frustrated I was.

I hated failure.

"Bel," he said when I didn't look up.

I kept my gaze firmly on the sandal, pretending to study it as if I could somehow change the outcome, though I knew for a fact I couldn't.

"Bel," he tried again, moving to sit beside me. "This is a good thing."

I scowled at him then. "How?"

"Now you know one of your limits." He spread his hands as if it were obvious. "You have to know these things to learn what you *can* do. Any mentor would tell you that."

I wrapped my arms around my legs and bit back the urge to say, *I wouldn't know.*

He reached out and tugged on the teal fabric of my gown, which hadn't changed. "As long as it's touching you, it sticks, right?" He didn't wait for an answer. "Maybe the change needs to be on something living? Change *my* sandals. See if it stays when you let go."

Despite the pit of doubt in my stomach, my spirits rose a little at his confidence in me. Maybe it wasn't *so* bad that he was here. Eyeing his sandals, which were as out of date as mine, I smirked. With only a tiny bit of effort, I turned them into furry snow boots instead.

The look on his face made me giggle.

"Hey!" he yelled, but then we realized at the same time that when I'd let go, they'd remained changed. He shook his head, but his tone was calmer as he grumbled, "I expect you to change those back."

"Take them off," I suggested instead, both curious and growing tired. I needed to reserve at least enough strength to return my dress back to normal before I went home.

I leaned forward as he tugged one of the boots off and set it in the same place I'd put my sandal. When it stood on its own, it once again reverted to its original form. Asher didn't waste any time yanking the other snow boot off to get his sandals back, strapping them on again hesitantly, almost as if he expected them to have a mind of their own.

With a sigh, I laid back on the grass and stared up at the faraway human-world version of the clouds.

Asher flopped down beside me, eyes soft, lips curled in a contented smile. "It's an incredible Gift," he whispered, though no one else was around. "Beautiful. Jinn are foolish to be afraid of it."

I blushed. Though I kept it from visibly reaching my cheeks, I couldn't quite stop myself from lowering my eyes to our hands between us.

He reached out, tangling his long fingers with mine, playing with them.

It was somehow more intimate than the kiss.

Another step across the invisible line between friends and something more.

But unlike the daleth, I didn't know if either of us were making it on purpose, or if it was inevitable. Something I'd wanted for so long that I didn't know what to do when it actually happened.

I closed my eyes and allowed a smile to touch my lips.

"I know what we could try!" His hand tightened on mine unexpectedly, startling me into looking over at him where he'd propped himself up on his elbow.

I couldn't explain why his expression made me hold my breath. But my heart began to race. As I sat up to listen, I subtly pulled my hand back into my lap. "Out with it, then."

Not letting me rush him, he merely leaned closer. "Since you've obviously been keeping this to yourself, I assume you haven't had a chance to try shifting someone else…"

Though it wasn't really a question, I shook my head, frowning. I didn't like where this was going.

He sat up and took my hand again, squeezing it with a gentle pressure as he said softly, "Bel, what if you could?" When I immediately started to shake my head, he squeezed harder, until it actually hurt. "Just think about it," he insisted. "Can you imagine all the things we could do? I can! The possibilities for power are practically limitless! What could it hurt to try?"

"Maybe tomorrow." I put him off. His interest in my Gift had been sweet at first, but for some reason it was starting to make me uncomfortable. Why was he so fascinated by it? Was I becoming another one of his enchanted items—another obsession? I shrugged off the uneasiness. This was Asher. We'd grown up together. I was probably reading too much into it.

Still, I needed time to think. Eventually, I just stood and said, "I have to get home before I'm missed."

CHAPTER 4

ASHER WASN'T ONE TO forget or let something go. He pestered me about going to the human world again the next afternoon, and the next, and the next. "I'll tell the others we're busy," he said when I protested that they'd try to come. "They know you like me." He winked, and I blushed before I could stop it. "I'll tell them I feel the same way, and we need some time alone."

Since my father worked late, I eventually gave in on the fourth day. The idea of changing Asher's form instead of my own was daunting, though. What if I wasn't capable?

On the other hand, what if I *could* learn, but without a mentor to teach me it would be impossible to figure it out on my own?

As he kissed me goodnight and reminded me again to meet him at the daleth tomorrow, there was also a tiny thought that I pushed to the back of my mind that asked, *What if I change him, but then I can't change him back?*

Still, it was Asher's choice to start with this. He could imagine the risks as well as I could.

With unspoken agreement, we met early the next afternoon and made our way through the daleth to the human side, to the clearing where we'd stood a few days prior.

Unlike last time, though, we were both quiet. Tense. No kissing or cuddling today, not with something this huge looming over us. Asher's usual pale skin seemed stark white against his standard day armor and tunic, and his throat bobbed nervously.

"You can change your mind," I offered. The first words we'd spoken since meeting.

He only shook his head. As if words were too much, and he might lose his nerve.

With a deep breath, I closed my eyes. I'd

worried about this for the last four days.

I'd decided to attempt a change that was similar to his current size.

A wolf.

Whether or not I needed to touch him was unclear. Pretending to be deep in thought, I imagined him shifting.

Nothing happened.

I hid my failure, though, feigning a new start, as I stepped up to him and took his hand.

Something about the contact told me instantly it would work this time.

He opened his mouth, probably to ask what was taking so long, but I'd already begun. Choking on whatever he'd been about to say, his eyes widened as his fingers transformed into a huge gray paw in my palm. Then his nose began to lengthen. Instinct made him lift a hand to his face, but instead of a hand he scratched his new gray muzzle with his other paw.

I tugged him down to the ground, keeping my hand on his hairy foreleg. This allowed him to stand on all fours while I finished the change down to the tail, making his clothes shift into nothing before they could rip, though I kept his red eyes the same.

In the span of a few short minutes, he'd metamorphosed into a powerful gray wolf.

Finished with the change, I let go. As I'd expected, the change in him was as permanent as it always was in me; a living body would always hold the new form. Part of me wanted to ask how he felt. Of course, that would be a waste of breath.

"Are you okay?" I whispered instead, as if anything louder might startle his animal nature.

Was he still himself, the way I was in animal form?

He dipped his big head in an exaggerated nod. A wolf-like grin appeared on his new face, tongue hanging out, sharp white fangs glinting in the light, ears up and relaxed as his red eyes danced.

With a soft growl that was almost a purr, he danced back, spun in a circle, and then without warning, took off.

"Wait!" I yelled, terrified that I'd been wrong. I'd thought for sure that was completely Asher beneath the new façade, but now I wasn't nearly as certain.

Already, I'd lost sight of him.

Branches tearing and sticks crunching beneath his feet grew softer as he put distance between us faster than I'd have thought possible.

What have I done?

Long minutes passed.

He didn't return.

I slowly moved in shock toward the log where we'd sat so happily only a few days prior and sank onto its rough surface.

This was it.

I'd be found out for sure now.

Mind racing, I frantically tried to think of what I could say to his parents. Maybe I could tell the Jinni Guard about the portal, and say he'd gone through it but never came back?

They didn't need to know the details, that would be enough. *Wouldn't it?*

Time dragged by.

Asher still didn't come back.

Shaking, I tried to tell my legs to stand and carry me back home, but I couldn't find the will to leave yet.

I shut my eyes, trying to hold in tears.

This was all my fault.

I should've told him *no*.

So engrossed was I in my dread that I didn't hear the softly padding footsteps until they stopped in front of me and a warm furry head dropped into my lap, poking a wet nose against my bare arm.

I screamed and fell backward off the log.

Asher—for, of course, the big gray wolf with impossible red eyes was Asher—yipped almost gleefully, jumping up over the log to run a circle around me as if my anxiety attack was entertaining to him.

"How *dare* you run off like that?" I yelled at him, forgetting myself for a moment as the fading adrenaline made my muscles weak. My panic at almost leaving him there turned into guilt. "I'm turning you back right now!"

With a whine, he tucked his tail between his legs and backed away from me.

Clearly pleading for more time.

Standing with precise movements to cover my embarrassment over being startled so easily, I brushed the twigs and dirt off my skirt and legs before I deigned to answer him, trying to hide how breathless I still felt. "Fine." I inhaled deeply and added, "But if you're not back within the next ten minutes, I swear I'll leave without you."

He bounded away without another sound, long legs launching him across the clearing and out of sight once more.

This time I buried the rising apprehension and began counting. I told myself I was only pacing out of boredom. My lungs were tight. This was too much responsibility. Like the first day he'd found out, I wished fervently that he'd never discovered my Gift and everything could go back to the way it used to be.

When he finally vaulted back over the log and into the clearing, panting hard, it was an effort to keep my spine straight and my face clear of emotion. I wouldn't reveal myself so easily again.

"Come," I motioned when he stopped out of reach. Bending, I touched his furry shoulder and began the process of changing him again, bringing back his original form—height, clothes, annoyingly persuasive voice, and all.

A gasp came from the forest behind me.

I spun to face the intruder.

Searching for a human, I was prepared to scare them into submission, but instead I froze at the familiar face.

Simon.

Why was he here? I couldn't find words as we stared at each other across the short distance. He kept glancing at Asher where he stood behind me and then back to me. Obviously, he'd seen everything.

I opened my mouth to call him over.

His eyes flew wide in alarm, and he flashed

away before I could say a word.

"Simon!" I yelled, not sure if he'd just traveled out of sight or if he was truly gone. "Simon, come back! I won't hurt you!"

"It's true, Simon!" Asher yelled too, as we each swiveled around, trying to spot him if he decided to reappear somewhere nearby. "She has to touch you to do anything. You're safe!"

As far as we know, I thought harshly. *But I'd make an exception for idiotic Simon, if I knew how.*

There was no response.

He must've truly left then. My heart sank. Had he gone back to the daleth? Was he telling everyone? When had he arrived and how much had he seen? Ice filled my veins. Even if he'd only caught the last few seconds, it was enough.

For the second time in less than the span of an hour, I feared the worst: I'd return home to find my father had disowned me, my friends would all fear me, and the Jinni Guard would press me into forced service with the threat of otherwise being put on a watch for my too-strong Gift.

"This is all your fault!" I whirled on Asher. "You told him we were here!"

It was only a guess, but he couldn't hide the guilt

that crossed his face. "I've been meeting him here every afternoon because you refused to come," he protested. "I'm sorry. I forgot to tell him not to come today! I tried to warn you that I smelled him as you changed me back, but it was too late." Despite everything falling apart around me, he had the audacity to grin. "That change was so incredible! I never would've imagined!"

Crossing my arms, I strode away, furious with myself for continuing to trust this stupid boy who'd taken advantage of me.

Asher caught up to me, apparently realizing he wasn't quite forgiven. "Bel, I truly am sorry. You have to believe me. Normally he and I meet on the other side of the daleth anyway; I never would've expected him to come to the human side without me. Still, it's my fault. We should've come farther in to be safe. I wish I could go back in time and stop it. If I had a Gift as powerful as yours I would. I'll—"

I stopped at the edge of the treeline, throwing my head back, eyes squeezed shut. "Stop." Some of the ferocity had drained from me, turning to a quiet despair instead. My life was over. "I know you didn't mean to. What's done is done."

Eventually, I began walking again, slower this time. Enough time had passed for Simon to tell a dozen Jinn by now.

The tiny bit of string that marked the portal fluttered in the wind, growing closer with each step. Part of me was tempted to just stay in the human world. It was dingy and savage, but at least no one could abuse my Gifts here.

Not for the first time, I wondered if that's exactly what my mother had done when she'd left years ago.

Without warning, Simon appeared through the portal a dozen paces ahead. On his heels were Miriam and Phillipa. All three of them stared at me as if I'd grown horns on my head.

I was tempted to check if I'd somehow done exactly that without conscious thought. But no. It was because he'd told them. Simon had described what he'd seen, and now all four of my friends knew my secret.

They stood tense and almost crouched, as if ready to spring away from me.

Instead of endeavoring to explain or calm them down, I burst into tears.

Hurriedly, I put my back to them, trying to stop the flow of raw emotion.

They hated me now.

I'd never be the same in their eyes. A small taste of what it'd be like to go home.

It crushed me.

Asher came to my side, trying to put his arm around my shoulders, but I shrugged him off.

I still blamed him for this. If not for him and his pressuring, I could've gone on the way I was for many more years, if not forever.

He sighed.

I didn't take my hands from my face, unwilling to let them see my lack of control.

When his shadow faded away, though, I wanted to call him back. I swiped at the tears on my cheeks.

Soft whispers floated toward me from him and the others, but I couldn't make anything out.

Shamelessly, I transformed the inner workings of my ears to be as sharp as an owl, allowing me to listen in without turning around or coming near them. It helped calm me a little.

"—like I said, she doesn't want anyone to know."

"Well, yeah." Simon scoffed, although with my attuned hearing I noticed his voice shook a little. "But Miriam and Phillipa have a right to know. And so do I." His voice grew loud enough that I would've heard it even with regular hearing, no doubt his intent. "She *should've* told us."

As I listened, a tiny spark of hope rose. Had he really not told anyone else? Just the girls?

I changed my hearing back to normal as I wiped the remaining tears from my cheeks and turned to face them. "Have you forgotten what my father is like?" I'd meant to put some force behind the words, but they were as dry and brittle as an old, fallen leaf. "You can't tell anyone." And though it hurt me to beg, I added softly, "Please."

Grudgingly, Simon crossed his arms and shrugged. "I haven't told on you yet, have I?"

That was the confirmation I'd so desperately needed. Despite myself, my shoulders sagged in relief. Still, I tilted my head toward Miriam and Phillipa, who'd remained at the very edge of the daleth, though they'd ceased to look scared of me. More curious really.

Simon scowled. "Like I said, they have the right to know. We all should know who we're spending our time with."

Pursing my lips, I hated how much this was out of my control. "We'll choose conflict, then," I ended the disagreement the way Jinn were often forced to. How extreme the conflict turned out to be was in his hands, as far as I was concerned.

Phillipa stepped forward, always the peacemaker. "Simon says you turned Asher into a beast? Can you do all manner of shape-shifting?"

I told them only what Asher already knew, and no more. Whenever I tried to hold back, he would fill in the blanks in excitement, either not catching my darting glances or choosing to ignore them.

"Lovely." Miriam's eyes narrowed on my face. "So you're one of the most powerful Jinn and you've been laughing at us poor fools behind our backs all this time."

"No!" I was quick to argue, though part of me perked up at the backhanded compliment. *Most powerful? Am I? Is that why Asher won't leave my side?* Out loud I only said, "I would never laugh at you. You are *all* my friends."

Though Miriam only crossed her arms, mimicking Simon's discomfort and Asher's frustration, Phillipa smiled and moved toward me, taking my hand before facing the others. "It'd be good to have a powerful friend," she said to me, though her tone said it was really to the others. "I, for one, am very pleased."

I squeezed her hand gratefully. The tears threatened again, and I had to blink to hold them back. Until now, I hadn't realized how much their friendship meant to me. But did I truly still have it?

Asher spoke up, "As you saw, Bel can change us as well as herself. I don't think any of you realize how powerful this is." He turned to me. "Even you, Bel. You're still treating it like a curse, instead of the Gift it is."

Standing there with three friends judging me, I only scowled at him and muttered under my breath, "If you had it, you wouldn't be so quick to say that."

But I knew that was a lie. He would've embraced it to the fullest. I had the one thing he'd always wanted desperately: real power.

"Think about it," he said, gesturing excitedly to me and the others, waving us closer, which we reluctantly obeyed. "Sure, it's fun to be an animal, and maybe use that transformation to hide from someone—" he waved in my direction "—such as a bad-tempered father." I refused to respond and he didn't really wait for one. "But the changes don't have to be so drastic. You could also shape-shift one of us to be taller or more handsome." He paused for dramatic effect, letting us imagine the little changes we all wanted. Glancing around at each of us, his gaze landed on me with a grin. "You could shape-shift into one of the Jinni Guards, or even a *royal*. Or, better yet—you could change *them*."

My jaw dropped.

Until Asher, I'd never allowed myself to consider what I could do to someone else, much less something as specific as that.

Not that transforming into someone else had much real use. Since I'd never met Prince Shem in person—very few in my social standing ever had—I doubted very much I could transform into him or anyone in the royal family based on a mere image on a coin or piece of paper.

Still… I reconsidered other possibilities. I had in fact already transformed into someone else—into a human, no less—our first night here in the human world. That had been *extremely* useful.

Their eyes were on me, waiting. But Asher had revealed enough of my secrets for one day. I needed to think things over on my own before anything else was shared.

"My father will be expecting me," I used the worn-out excuse gratefully. "We can talk more about it another time, if we must. I have to go."

"Come on, Bel," Asher pressed, stepping up to me, lowering his voice to a whisper between the two of us. "Just promise me you'll think about it?"

I nodded, and when he ushered all of us back through the daleth, he said in a firm tone, "We'll meet here again tomorrow evening. Same place."

I wondered if I really had a choice anymore.

CHAPTER 5

I APPROACHED THE DALETH with heavy footsteps. Not only was I late, but for the thousandth time I contemplated not going at all. If only Asher hadn't seen me. If only the others hadn't found out. If only I didn't have this Gift in the first place.

My mother had been right. *People only want to use you.* And foolish girl that I am, I'd given them something to use. I should've pretended with Asher that I couldn't change him, but I'd wanted to know for myself.

Now, if I didn't show, there was a chance—however big or small I wasn't sure—that one of my friends would rat me out to the Jinni Guard or my own father.

I didn't know which was worse.

Closing my eyes against the worry, I forced myself to step through the portal into the human world.

Bird song greeted me, cheerful and carefree. Completely discordant with my current mood. Other than the wind blowing through the trees, I didn't sense anything. The others must be in the little clearing already.

A small part of me hoped that somehow they'd all stayed home. But as I thought this, laughter reached me through the trees. Muffled voices.

Though I did my best to approach silently, their conversation died off when they spotted me. Already our friendship had changed, maybe forever.

"We're all a little nervous." Asher swung his arm over my shoulder. I appreciated him trying to pretend the tension wasn't my fault. Normally it'd make me smile, but today it barely broke through my attentiveness. I was too busy watching the other's reactions to me, looking for any warning signs. He added, "We decided we want to go back to the human town… and try being humans for a day."

When his words hit me, I pulled back. "What?

Why?"

Grinning, Asher shook his head. "I'll tell all of you when we get there."

I expected one of the others to put up a fight, especially Miriam, who always argued against Asher's ridiculous schemes. Instead, she stepped forward, surprising me with an unexpected request. "I was thinking…" She hesitated, then spoke in a rush, "Can you make us look like anything at all?"

Biting my lip, I slowly nodded. "I think so…"

Miriam's thin face lit up. She touched her nose and eyes self-consciously and whispered her requests in my ear. The tip of her nose came to a long point, could I make it softer? Her dull blue eyes were her next request. They were both too large for the rest of her face and too human in color for a Jinni.

"That's what we want right now though," I whispered back. "All of us need to have human-colored eyes."

Reluctantly, she nodded. Glancing over her shoulder at the others, she softly asked, "Can you enhance them when we come back home, then? And if you do, will it stick?"

Once again, my spine stiffened at the assumption that I'd simply agree.

Miriam's normally flat, insolent expression was

for once bright and hopeful as she gazed up at me.

Some of my tension faded. I could understand wishing to be different. After all, hadn't I just yesterday added enhancements to my own features? Sighing, I agreed.

With those requests out of the way, she let me remake her short dress in the longer human fashion without comment, and when she turned back to the others, she was a different person—not only on the outside, but inside too. Her smile lit up her entire face. Even if I hadn't changed her nose per her request, she'd have been stunning, though of course, she'd never believe me if I said so.

"I don't want you to change anything except my clothes," Simon snapped as he stepped forward next, not moved in the slightest by Miriam's unusual excitement.

I crossed my arms.

"Simon, be reasonable." Asher stepped between us before my glare could turn into anything more. "You have to at least change your eyes." He waved to Simon's iridescent green, common in Jinn but an otherworldly shade for humans. "We're trying to blend in, remember?"

"Fine." Simon braced himself, lip curled in

disgust.

His dislike of being touched by me was the biggest issue; every time I tried to start shifting him, he jerked back, and the shifting stopped. "Hold still!"

Though he continued to squirm, I tried to make quick work of his eyes and clothes, lengthening the tunic but not bothering to do much more, wanting to be done with him as much as he wanted to be done with me.

Asher was next, and I did the same changes for him that I'd done for Simon, giving all of us brown eyes and simple clothes. Though he squeezed my fingers and gave me a comforting smile, that old sensation of butterflies was missing.

We each removed some of our more decorative outerwear—arm bands, belts, hair pieces, and shoulder drapings—and tucked them in a small groove beneath the daleth tree. This allowed me to save my energy. Though I didn't reveal it to the others, these more minor changes barely made a dent in my strength.

Phillipa pulled me aside, waiting for the others to stop paying attention—which happened quickly as they admired each other's new features—before she timidly asked, "Could you make me taller? And maybe stronger?" Unlike Miriam, I knew immediately she wasn't asking for these changes out of vanity. The last time we'd been here had left its mark.

"Of course," I agreed immediately. Shifting her soft, yellow eyes into the same human shade of brown as everyone else was quick. With some difficulty, I also played with the round, innocent shape of her face to make it narrower and less trusting. Without a visual to base it on, it was like creating art from scratch, and it took a couple tries before I surreptitiously based it on the way Simon was glowering at me. Then, finally, it looked natural.

Giving her additional height forced me to exert myself in a different way. Taller was taller, but it took more energy. Adding muscle definition, especially to her arms, which I left bare in her new gown, proved to be the most simple of the changes she'd requested.

When I finished, she flexed them in awe, standing taller for the first time in weeks. Maybe months. I hadn't realized how much she'd slouched before, as if trying to hide within herself.

For the first time since this whole experience began, I was happy to use my Gift for someone else.

This time when we entered the town on the busy

main road, the sun was nearing the horizon and there were humans everywhere.

Everywhere.

Without meaning to, we all froze at the outskirts like deer caught in a hunter's gaze.

The humans didn't even notice us.

Going about their evening, they moved at different speeds or not at all. Some were leaving town on the main road, while others were just arriving. They filled the air with yelling as they tried to sell their wares, while banging and hammering sounded from down the street, and children squealed as they raced past us in a group with a leathery ball made out of an animal intestine.

Such a primitive culture.

"Get out of the way!" a deep voice yelled, making all of us jump and then hurry to the side of the road as a driver prodded his horse and cart forward.

"Where to?" I asked Asher, since this was after all, his idea.

He blinked his now dull-brown eyes, unsure.

Pointing to a sign partway down the road, he said, "I think that's a human tavern? Why don't we try one of their drinks?"

"We don't have any money," Miriam reminded

him, but without her usual malice. She was smiling at the humans who passed by us, and beaming when some of them smiled back.

"I'll handle that," Simon said, disappearing from the middle of our group without warning.

"Fool!" Asher hissed under his breath, as all of us scanned the crowd in a hurry, worried that a human had seen.

We didn't need to start rumors of Jinn in this town. We weren't supposed to be here. And forget the reaction of the Jinni Guard back home, the humans were more dangerous to us than most realized. They had far superior numbers to our five. Or, four now.

When Simon reappeared in the exact same place, we were ready this time, standing in a protective circle, acting as nonchalant as possible. We wildly speed-read the passersby again to make sure no one noticed.

An *oof* sounded behind me, and I turned back to find Simon doubled over, clutching his stomach. "What was that for?" he groaned to Asher.

"Next time you're stupid enough to travel in broad daylight for no good reason, you're done," Asher's voice was low and furious, enunciating every word. "Is that clear?"

"Done?" Simon tried to joke, wincing as he stood back up. "With what?"

"All of it," Asher said in a flat tone, not smiling back. "Us. Coming here. You make a move like that again, and you're out."

"Fine." Simon scowled. He held out a little brown bag and shook it, making whatever was inside clink together. "Sounds like you don't want the money I got us then."

Phillipa and I glanced at each other, and she was the first to ask, anxiously, "Simon, what did you do?"

"Don't worry about it," he waved a hand at her, smiling again as if he thought she was impressed. "The human won't wake up for hours. By then we'll be long gone."

Asher didn't praise him, but he didn't chastise him again either. Instead, he turned on his heel, leading the way toward the tavern he'd pointed out earlier, and the others followed.

I trailed along behind them, staring at their backs. What Simon had done technically broke the Unbreakable Laws. Even if it was a minor infraction, being that it was a human. So, why didn't they fear Simon and his Gift, but they feared me? What made me so different in their eyes? Though I was with them now, it wasn't the same. Sometimes I'd catch them looking at me strangely. And now, as we entered the dimly lit tavern, none of them seemed to care if I followed or not.

We sat at the closest open table, furtively glancing around at the mostly empty room. Was this not a good tavern?

Near the back, a human wearing an apron wove through the tables toward us.

I leaned forward and hissed, "Who's going to talk to the human?"

"Not me," Miriam said immediately, and both Phillipa and Simon were quick to agree.

"I vote you," Asher said to me. "You can use your Gift to calm her or something."

"It's shape-shifting, not *hypnotism*," I snapped, but I didn't have time to say anything else.

"Welcome to the New Kings Inn," the woman intoned. "What'll you have?"

Panicking, I pointed to the only other table with customers and blurted out. "We'll have what they're having."

She swiveled to look at their food: three drinks and three big plates filled with meat and bread. Turning back to me, brows raised, she asked, "Will that be for you alone or for the whole table?"

"All of us," I said quickly, wanting her gone as soon as possible. I took the little purse from Simon's hand and emptied the coin onto the sticky wooden surface. "Will this be enough?"

She blinked at me, raised brows coming together suspicously. "That's more than enough, honey. I only need six of those."

"Sorry," I laughed a little breathlessly, waving a hand as if embarrassed. "I'm a little distracted."

She studied me as I counted them out and handed the coins over. With a shrug, she moved away to help another table of customers that had just sat down, saying over her shoulder, "I'll tell the cook."

I awkwardly began returning the rest of the coins to the bag.

"That's not enough for all of us," Asher whispered as soon as she'd taken a few steps.

"If you wanted something different, you should've done it yourself," I hissed back, embarrassed. Tossing the coin bag across the table to Simon, I added, "You'd better return the rest of these to whoever you stole them from."

None of us mentioned that returning some but not all was still breaking one of the Unbreakable

Laws. It irked me, but I couldn't say anything further. It was too late. I'd already participated in breaking it simply by being present.

Simon rolled his eyes, but agreed. Underneath his cocky demeanor, he was as spooked as the rest of us, jiggling his leg nervously as he took in the dark room.

Phillipa usually didn't speak in large crowds, but she surprised all of us by leaning across the table, saying to Asher, "I think it's time you tell us why we're here."

His throat bobbed wildly as he swallowed. Glancing around the room, he leaned in too, waiting for all of us to do the same, before he whispered, "I want to steal one and bring them home."

"What?" I forgot to be quiet in my horror.

It took the others a few seconds longer to understand what he meant when he said *one*: a human.

Powerful Jinn sometimes enchanted humans with certain talents and brought them back to Jinn to work for them. No doubt Asher thought possessing a human would give him the same suggestion of power.

"Absolutely not." I moved my chair back to get

up and leave.

Asher grabbed my wrist, and Simon put a hand on the back of my chair, helping him keep me there. "Don't make a scene, Bel."

Yanking my hand back, I rubbed my wrist, which stung. The surprise of it brought tears to my eyes. I blinked them back. For the first time since I'd met Asher, I hated his lust for power.

"She's right though," Miriam said, taking my side, though she looked put out by it. "There's no way we could kidnap a human without leaving some trace. Do you think everyone back home is just going to accept that *you* have a human worker, without asking questions? The Jinni Guard would find out within the day, and you'd get the rest of us in trouble with you."

"The Jinni Guard does it all the time themselves," Simon argued, clearly intrigued by the idea. He still held my chair, though I hadn't moved.

I crossed my arms, fury boiling over. "If you even *consider* making me an accomplice in this, I swear on all of Jinn that I'll turn you into a frog for these humans' table."

The waitress set down a plate of froglegs on the table next to us right then, adding weight to my threat.

Asher scowled at me.

The others glanced between us, paler than normal, and didn't say a word.

If someone had asked me in that moment why I liked him, I wouldn't have been able to think of a reason. Right now, I didn't feel like I knew him at all, and I didn't want to.

More customers came in and the waitress forgot about us for a while as she took more and more orders. It seemed the dinner rush had begun.

When our food finally arrived, I couldn't even taste it. We were literally surrounded by humans. It was like going into the lair of one of the ugliest, most dangerous Lacklores wearing only a thin Lacklore hide, and hoping they didn't notice and eat us.

Asher still hadn't responded.

Something between us had shifted, and not in a good way.

"This drink isn't bad," Simon said, trying to pretend everything was fine. "If you get past that bitter taste."

"Let's just get out of here," I said, skin crawling with the sense of a hundred eyes on us.

Phillipa was quick to agree. "I don't know if I can last much longer. This many of them is too much."

But it was Miriam who finally convinced Asher to let go of his schemes. She put a hand on his arm, and said, "This town isn't going anywhere. If you're determined to pull off something like this, at least take the time to plan and do it right, so you don't get caught."

His glare scared off the humans around us, but he conceded with a short nod.

We left the half-eaten food and dregs of the drinks behind, scurrying out of the tavern on each other's heels.

Outside, I sucked in a deep breath of fresh air as we waited in an alley for Simon to return the remaining coins.

Without a word, we made our way through the streets, which were much quieter now, toward the edge of town. The sky was dark with the first stars beginning to twinkle. We'd lasted longer than I'd thought. Still, I'd put up more of a fight before coming here next time. I'd had enough of Asher's foolishness.

Glancing over at him, it was clear he was still holding a grudge against me as well. He wouldn't meet my eyes, and his fists were clenched.

We picked up our hair pieces, arm bands, belts,

and drapings, and crossed through the daleth before remembering to change out of our human forms.

Asher demanded I change him and Simon back first, and then they traveled away immediately, not waiting for the rest of us.

Miriam stopped me after I'd changed her dress back to normal. "Could you—" she hesitated with Phillipa right there—"could you let me keep a bit of the new nose?" she reminded me, as if worried I'd forgotten. "And maybe make my eyes a little more, you know, Jinni? Nothing obvious, of course, just a little bit brighter?"

As a friend, I couldn't find a reason to say no. It seemed cruel when it was within my grasp. So I did as she asked.

When she stepped back, Phillipa took her place, meeting my eyes. "I know keeping this height and these muscles is asking too much," she began. "Someone would notice. But, perhaps, I could keep the smallest amount today, and maybe add a little more every so often, over time?"

Once again, how could I say no? I understood why she wished for this completely. Her father and mine were so similar; they could have been best friends. I did as she asked, although I didn't leave much behind visibly. Still, the strength beneath the remaining muscles would serve her well.

"I'm so tired," I tell them as I finish, eyes drooping, body sagging. I couldn't remember the last time I spent this much of my Gift in such a short amount of time and with such precision. Detailed work took more out of me than I'd expected.

"I'll take Miriam home," Phillipa offered, since Miriam hated being forced to walk. "You get some rest."

Nodding, I traveled straight home, dragging myself up the stairs of the acropolis, sneaking inside, and falling into bed exhausted before I remembered to shift myself back as well.

Snores came from the outer room, but for once I was too tired to care. Pulling the blankets over me, I fell asleep instantly.

* * *

The next day, I ignored Asher's note to meet them at the daleth.

I was done going to the human world. Done doing favors for them. Done being used.

"Jezzie, where's the food?" my father yelled, pulling me out of my dark thoughts.

Asher knew better than to stop by when my

father was around, so for a while, I was left alone.

But he must've been watching the acropolis closely, because the following morning he came knocking right after my father went to work.

CHAPTER 6

"I JUST NEED A small favor," he said, before I'd even opened the door fully. The morning sun cast him in a glowing light that made him look far more innocent than he was.

No, *where have you been?* Or, *are you okay?* after I didn't show yesterday. Hot frustration seeped into my blood, making me spin away from him and stalk across the small room to the kitchen window.

Behind me, the door clicked shut. "I wouldn't ask if I wasn't desperate," Asher continued, as determined as always. "It's, well, I have this idea… It might be stupid."

It probably is.

When I glanced at him over my shoulder, his head was bowed and he scratched the back of his neck, staring at the fading paint on the wall.

Sighing, I pulled a wobbly chair out from the little table and sat. "What is it?"

Instead of sitting, he started to pace. To the kitchen window, back to the door, and over again. "It's not a big deal, really... After you changed our clothes that day, I was thinking of all the other things you could change. Or—" he corrected himself "—more specifically, what you could change them *into*."

He yanked a chair out from the table and dropped into it, leaning toward me. "Like coin."

Already shaking my head, I reminded him, "It isn't alive. It won't stay transformed on its own. You know that."

One side of his mouth tilted up. "It doesn't have to last, it only has to fool someone for a minute, then you slip the money in a coin purse before you let go." When I started shaking my head again, he spoke faster. "Come on, Bel!" He gave me that smirk that he knew full well had always worked for him before. "It just has to be an item that sounds similar when you shake the bag full of them. Maybe tin... or rocks... or maybe even shekels!"

Shekels were so small in value that they were often tossed in the street for orphans or beggars to pick up, since you'd need hundreds to buy something as simple as a loaf of bread.

While I had to admit, if only to myself, that the idea intrigued me, it was too risky. "There's no way. We'd get caught."

"Well, that's the best part." Asher grinned, almost as if he'd expected me to say that. "With your shape-shifting Gift, you can pretend to be anyone you want. After you use the fake coin and purchase this item for me, you can simply return to yourself. So, it has to be you, see?" He leaned back in the rickety wooden chair; the certainty of his control over me reminded me of my father.

"No," I bit out. He'd made me part of his schemes against my will too many times. Pressuring me to show him my Gift, to use it on him, attempting to steal a human—all of those instances were frustrating, but they were nothing compared to what he was asking now. "This isn't a game. This is my life. I'm not going to risk it."

"Listen, I didn't want to say this but... if you want me to keep your Gift a secret, then I need you to do this for me."

My freedom leeched away from me as quickly

as the blood drained from my face.

Quicker even, since it'd been gone the moment Asher walked into the room.

He wasn't giving me a choice. I hadn't had a choice since the moment he'd found out, and if he had his way, I'd *never* have one again.

The sharp stab of betrayal was almost physical. It made me breathless. Unable to speak.

Years of practice hiding my emotions from my father helped me keep my face calm even while breaking inside.

This was *Asher*.

I'd *trusted* him.

I took a mental step back, behind my old, familiar wall of secrets, building it back up in my mind.

I'd been a fool to think he cared for me.

When I could trust my voice enough to speak, I asked in a flat tone, "What is this 'item' you need so desperately?"

Asher grinned and leaned forward, assuming he'd hooked me into his schemes like he always did. "It's a lamp. About yea high—" he gestured a small distance between his palms "—with a solid gold base and a green, glass-blown top. Lamech just put it on sale yesterday."

"And what's so special about it?" I crossed my arms.

"It's spelled for travel."

Enchanted items and other tokens often enhanced Jinni Gifts. "I'm guessing it's meant to take Jinn further than they could naturally travel on their own?"

"Yes," he admitted. "But, think about it, Bel. Enchanted objects will also give you a Gift you *don't even have*!"

Ah. It all made sense now. He'd always been jealous that the rest of us—well, excluding Miriam—could travel, when he couldn't. It was such a common Gift that almost every Jinni had it, to some degree. Walking to a place like the daleth could take him an hour, while it took me only a split second to travel.

I was tempted to poke at him and his sensitivity. But I knew from experience that would only make him dig in his heels more.

"Come on, Bel," he said again, leaning forward to take my hand, a gesture that would've given me butterflies in the past. Rubbing his thumb against my skin, he added softly, "It's really not a big deal."

I sat there, speechless. He wanted me to use my

Gift in public, lie to a vendor who we both knew was going through difficult times, and steal from him. It was a *very* big deal. No. Absolutely not.

Patting the table, Asher stood, taking my silence as agreement. "I'd better go before your father gets back, or risk you having to turn me into one of your lizard creatures so I can escape."

I didn't laugh with him.

At the door, he paused with his fingers on the handle. "Oh, can you do it as soon as possible, though? I don't want someone else to snatch the lamp up just because we were slow. I can meet you this afternoon, after you pick it up—either here, or maybe out by the daleth?"

I still hadn't answered, seated in the same frozen position at the table. Had my *no* not been clear? I stared at him.

He waited patiently, as if expecting me to come to terms with his plan. Beneath his small smile though, his eyes were sharp.

"Was anything between us ever real?" I whispered finally. "Or, was it all a lie?"

"Don't be ridiculous." Asher laughed. "Nothing's changed. You're making this into something much larger than it really is."

"Then why the threats?"

He rubbed his forehead with a sigh. "You're so dramatic. It's not a threat. It's a fair trade."

I just shook my head wordlessly. He could spin anything. There was no reasoning with him.

"You know I'm right," he said when he glanced up at my expression. "You *have* to use your Gift. I'm *helping* you use it, one way or the other. With a mentor, or—" he smirked a little, pointing to himself "—better yet, with me."

When he'd said he'd turn me in, he'd meant it. He could call it a favor or a threat, but it didn't matter. If he didn't act on it this time, I had no doubt he would later. Whenever it suited his purposes.

I needed some leverage on him, or this would never end.

"So…" he dragged out the word when I still didn't say anything. "Should I meet you here in a couple hours?"

"No," I snapped. "Never come here again."

I hoped he'd hear the warning in my tone, but if he did, he chose to ignore it. "All right, daleth it is," he said as he stepped into the hall. "See you in a few hours." And he had the audacity to wink at me before he closed the door.

The walls that had always been my prison

seemed like nothing now in comparison to the prison of my own skin.

Once again, I walked through the chain of events that had brought me here in my mind, struggling to find the moment that I could've escaped this destination.

I couldn't find one.

My feet moved with a mind of their own.

Stopping in front of my tiny mirror in my bedroom, I shifted slowly. Carefully.

I became male, changing my clothes to fit my new form.

Taller. Shaggy dark hair. Deepening my voice until it matched the rest of my changes. A voice I knew well enough to form a close resemblance.

And red eyes.

Then, picking up my coin purse, which was empty, I left the acropolis and traveled to a quiet alley right outside the emporium, taking every precaution possible to make sure no one would see me and connect the dots. Better to be overly cautious than to *ever* be caught again.

I bent down until I'd collected a handful of shekels, listening to them clink together in the purse.

Then, I practiced. A dozen times, and a dozen

times more. Reaching into the purse, I shifted the small shekels into hefty gold coins the second I touched them, pulling them out to display them in my palm before quickly returning them to the bag.

Of course, the moment I let go, the metal returned to its original form.

The timing would have to be perfect.

"Asher!" the storekeeper called to me as I entered his store and the bell rang out. Lamech knew both of us in passing, which meant my impression of Asher had to be as accurate as possible.

I imitated his cocky stride, flinging my shoulders back and grinning, ignoring the way my heart pounded. This next part would be the true test. I had to speak. "I'm here about the lamp from the other day."

Lamech's brows rose, but his weak yellow eyes were pleased. "I didn't expect you to come back so soon. You understand, the price hasn't changed?"

Clearly, he didn't think Asher had the money.

And technically, he'd be right.

A nagging feeling that this was going to make things worse instead of better tickled my neck, but I wasn't about to turn back now. Taking out my coin purse, I smoothly changed the coins as I pulled them out. A spirit of showmanship struck me. I flaunted each coin, dropping it back into the coin purse one at a time, counting each one—careful to let go only once they were out of sight.

The *clink, clink, clink* made the storekeeper's small smile grow wide.

I tightened the string and tossed the little purse on the counter in front of him. This was yet another opportunity to fail, as he only needed to double check the coins to discover the truth.

Keeping my body relaxed and my smile in place, I waited.

Brows still raised, Lamech turned to the shelf behind his counter, where the more valuable items were kept.

Though there were multiple lamps, he didn't ask which one, just gently took down a small glass-blown lamp—with a gold base and a deep green glass bulb, exactly like Asher had described.

Clearly, Asher had made his desires known the last time he'd been here.

"You're very lucky," he told me as he placed the lamp on the counter. It was the size of my palm. "More than a few others have eyed this today. I was considering raising the price."

I put two fingers on the little coin bag and thrust

it across the counter toward him. "Good thing you didn't yet," I replied in a flat tone.

Fortunately for me, that's exactly what Asher would've done, so Lamech only huffed as he pulled out a paper to write a receipt.

I took the lamp and the receipt, thanking him, and walked out.

If I traveled away from his shop's doorstep, it would be a dead giveaway that it wasn't Asher. Not to mention, it'd leave a trail to follow that would lead to me instead of him, so I continued walking instead. All the way to the other side of the emporium, and on toward the river, until there was not another soul in sight.

Only there, did I finally travel.

I didn't go straight home then either, but instead traveled to the daleth and entered the human world.

Inspiration struck me.

Though I couldn't travel just anywhere in the human town without being spotted, there was one dark little cranny I was familiar with, that—if I visited—no one else would see.

I lay down on the grass to be in the necessary position, and traveled there.

Opening my eyes, I blinked up at the wooden frame of the bed and the straw mattress above me.

Little Naseem's bed in the human house.

To one side was a wall, and to the other, bare feet under a dress moved about the room, unaware of my presence.

I only needed a moment. I silently set the lamp down beneath the bed, where it might easily go undiscovered for years, before traveling back to the daleth and re-entering Jinn.

From there, I made three more stops in the woods to hide my trail more thoroughly, before I finally traveled back into the hall of the acropolis.

I listened at the door, making sure my father wasn't home yet, and stepped inside before I finally remembered to shift back into my own form.

Even when everything was returned to normal, I didn't recognize the girl in the mirror. Something about her had changed.

I couldn't look too long.

Guilt nagged at me, overcoming the initial satisfaction as I hurried to finish my chores before my father came home.

Asher would absolutely hate me for what I'd done. But he would take the hint and leave me alone.

At least, that's what I kept telling myself.

He *had* to.

Belatedly, his other possible reactions flitted through my mind. Ones I hadn't let myself consider before... *No. It's too late now.* There was no taking it back. I convinced myself that it'd had to be done.

I couldn't let them exert this pressure over me anymore. I refused.

CHAPTER 7

YET, WHEN A FIST pounded on the door a few hours later, I somehow expected it. Only two Jinni I knew behaved like that. And my father had no reason to knock.

Asher burst in as soon as the lock turned. "What have you done?" he screamed in my face. His red eyes burned like a hot fire and his face was flushed.

Though I tried not to react, when he slammed the door behind him, I instinctively stepped back.

When my father got like this, I hid. As long as I was out of sight, he left me alone.

But Asher wasn't going to let me out of his sight.

He grabbed my wrist, twisting painfully. "You used my face!" he shouted. "You knew they'd come after me as soon as they found out—if I had been home, I'd have been caught! You have to fix this!"

Swallowing hard, I tried to pull my arm away, but he only gripped tighter. "I thought you'd get the message," I tried to snap back but my voice shook. "You can't control me anymore."

"No," Asher growled, yanking me forward and grabbing my other arm, putting pressure on them until I stopped struggling. "Unless you want everyone to know your precious secret, you will fix this. Now!"

I would never know how exactly he'd wanted me to do that.

With my hands pressed so tightly together, it only took a small, excruciating twist of my wrist to touch his hand.

When my fingers touched his skin, his eyes widened in understanding.

"No—" he gasped, trying to let go and back away, but now I grabbed *him* and held on, shapeshifting him as fast as my ability would allow.

In seconds, he shrunk down to just a few fingers tall.

Turned green and leathery.

And grew a tail.

In his new lizard form, he scurried across the floor, trying to escape me, but I pressed down on him with both hands, trapping him.

When I picked him up, his frantic struggles scratched my hands, drawing blood. I ran to the kitchen, dumping a jar of flour into the sink and tossing him inside.

But the lid didn't have any air holes.

Biting my lip, I tried to think. There was a matching lid on the sugar jar. Taking it off, I put my hand to it and attempted to use my Gift. It felt foreign. Wrapping my fingers around it, I tried harder, and managed to shift the metal just enough so that it had holes. But the moment I let go, they disappeared.

This Gift was *useless*!

Asher had stopped struggling. His lizard form sagged inside the glass jar as he slowly began to run out of air.

"Hold on," I murmured. I couldn't let him die.

Shifting the lid again, I put a knife in the hole before I let go this time. Then, once it had closed in around the knife, I yanked it out. A tiny hole stayed in place. I did this three more times, hoping that would be enough airholes, then hurried to switch the lids.

After a few moments of fresh air, Asher's tiny green body twitched.

I breathed a sigh of relief.

Replacing the sugar jar back in the cupboard and flushing the tell-tale flour down the sink, I took the jar that now formed Asher's prison to my room. Setting him on my tiny dresser, I fell back on the bed and dropped my head in my hands.

The full magnitude of what I'd done hit me.

I'd gone too far.

No matter what angle I approached it from, there was no coming back from this.

If Asher returned to his own form, he would turn me in and I'd be thrown in the castle dungeon. If he didn't, I had no doubt they'd come looking for him, discover what I'd done, and I'd *still* be caught and thrown in the dungeon.

This was exactly why the Unbreakable Laws had been created.

And somehow I'd broken all of them in just a few hours. I'd deceived. Stolen. And now harmed.

When I raised my head, Asher's stare pierced me, somehow conveying fury and disgust even in lizard form.

I stood just long enough to shove my single picture frame of my mother in front of the jar. Turning off the light, I crawled into bed and closed my eyes. I would figure this out in the morning.

Long after my father came home drunk in the middle of the night, I still lay wide awake. My mind held onto the problem relentlessly, trying to untie it, like an impossible knot.

Very few ideas came to me.

Those that did were too dark to consider.

I didn't know what to do or who to ask. I couldn't trust anyone.

The next morning, I didn't get out of bed.

I'd barely slept.

When the front door slamming shut signaled my father leaving for work, I could've gotten up, but I only checked that Asher was still breathing before I curled up in bed once more.

I stared at the square of sunlight all morning as it crept across my room.

Afternoon passed even more slowly.

A knock on the door made me frown. Was I supposed to be somewhere? I ran a brush through my hair and straightened the clothes I hadn't bothered to take off yesterday before I answered.

A Jinni Guard with icy blue eyes and full body armor designed for actual battle not just for looks stood on the other side. "Is the head of the household available?"

I shook my head. "I can give him the message?"

He ignored my answer. "Are you one of the companions of Asher, son of Methuselah, son of Obed?"

I didn't know what to say, so I just nodded. The members of the Jinni Guard were by far the most Gifted in all of Jinn, and rumor had it some had the rare Gift of Conviction: the ability to spot the difference between a lie and the truth. Every word had to be chosen carefully. "Is he... okay?"

"We are uncertain. He has been reported missing and is wanted for some possible criminal activity. We are speaking with friends and family to ascertain his whereabouts."

Nodding slowly, I put a hand to my heart. Body language wasn't usually as readable as words. I couldn't say, 'I hope you find him,' or, 'I'll keep an eye out for him,' because those would both be lies. "Let me know when you find him?" I asked instead, squinting my eyes and trying to seem sincere.

The guard gave a sharp bow. "My name is

Eliezer, son of Japeth, son of Hezekiah. If you come across any new information, come find me immediately. I'll be sure to follow up if I have further questions."

Not at all what I'd asked.

As he turned his back, I shut the door, trying to discern if he was onto me or simply following protocol.

My stomach growled loudly. Now that he'd pulled me out of my stupor, I realized I was starving.

All we had was some stale bread and cheese. Scraping the mold off, I ate all of it. My father rarely ate at home, but I decided to go pick up more food just in case.

The short trip to the emporium gave me a chance to clear my head and get some distance from Asher, whose presence I could feel everywhere in our little apartment.

When I came back, I had yet to come up with an idea, but I thought I could at least talk to Asher and explain myself, even if he couldn't talk back. Maybe he might be in a better mindset today. Maybe there was still a way out of this.

I finished putting the food away right when someone knocked on the door again. The guard was back already? Was that a bad sign or a good one?

Wiping my suddenly sweaty hands on my dress, I cleared my throat and swung the door open. "Simon?" My heart did an erratic dance. "What are you doing here?"

He pushed past me, eyes searching the small room and its few hiding places. "Is Asher here?" he asked, turning to me. His eyes were narrowed. Wary. "He was supposed to meet me, but he didn't show. Last I heard, he was with you."

I widened my eyes and shrugged. "I haven't seen him. What's going on?" Simon didn't have any truth-seeking Gifts, so I didn't hesitate to deny I knew anything to him.

It turned out that was a mistake.

"A member of the guard was just at my place," he said in a low, dangerous tone. "He said he came here first. I'd hoped I was wrong about my suspicions, but you obviously know something. Where is he?"

"I swear I don't." I spread my hands wide. "He's clearly not here. You can see for yourself."

I'd hoped he wouldn't take me up on it, but I could not be so lucky.

"I'll do that," he snapped, whirling around to stalk across the room, checking behind the low furniture. He opened the one cupboard large enough to fit a Jinni, then stalked toward my room.

Even before he pushed open the door, I knew what I had to do.

This time, I didn't hesitate.

By the time his eyes landed on the jar, where Asher was scratching at the glass walls in warning, my hand was on Simon's back, and he was shrinking.

Becoming a lizard too.

Darker green this time, so I could tell them apart.

Joining Asher in the little glass jar with air holes.

Just like Asher had, he clawed the sides, desperately trying to escape, while his friend looked on in resignation.

"I'm sorry," I whispered, struggling not to cry— not just for them, but also for myself and my own stupidity getting into this mess. "I didn't want to. You have to believe me. But I can't let you turn me in."

CHAPTER 8

THE NEXT DAY, I woke up with grim determination for what I had to do. It had been an impossible choice. My friends, or my freedom. My innocence, or my future. But really, hadn't it already been made? At this point, my only choice was to finish carrying it out.

I was ready.

With careful efforts, I sat in front of my little mirror and created dark circles under my eyes, rumpling my clothes and hair. I even tested my Gift to see if it could form tears on command. It would take more practice, but I thought eventually I could figure it out.

Phillipa knocked on my door first, around mid-afternoon. I leaned my forehead against the wall, taking a deep breath to bolster my resolve. I'd desperately hoped Miriam would be the one to come. It would've made this easier. Though not by much.

Still, I followed the plan I'd come up with the night before. "We can't talk here," I whispered as soon as I cracked open the door, pretending to look over my shoulder as if my father was asleep in the room behind me, though in truth, it was empty. "Meet me at the daleth—on the human side—in a half-hour. Tell Miriam too."

Two of them would be more difficult than one. I'd eaten a huge meal and slept late into the morning in an attempt to prepare. I knew my extra training lately had strengthened my Gift, but by how much, I couldn't say. There was only one way to find out.

When the girls came through the daleth, I stood trembling on the human side with my bag on my shoulder. I pressed my hands together against my body to hide the shaking. Beneath them, my stomach churned, threatening to bring up everything I'd eaten earlier. *It has to be done,* I repeated to myself, as I had all day.

Inside my bag was a second, empty glass jar

with airholes.

"I think Asher may have come to the human world to hide," I tell them my pre-rehearsed story, urging those tears to come. It doesn't quite work, I still need to see myself in a mirror to manipulate them. But by their worried reactions, my anxiety is enough. "I'll explain everything, but first we should search for him. Let's spread out. Meet back here by the portal in a quarter hour."

They were quick to agree. Anything for Asher. Bitterness twisted in me, wondering if they'd have done the same for me. Had any of us ever truly been friends?

I brushed aside the guilt nagging at me for what I was about to do, as we each went in a separate direction.

As soon as I was hidden by the trees, I looped back around to follow Miriam, traveling short distances to catch up to her, moving as silently as possible.

She never saw me coming.

Scooping up the little pink and orange lizard, I unscrewed the lid of the jar and gently set her inside, whispering apologies, though I knew they didn't mean much.

I used the remaining time to capture crickets,

adding them to the jar with Miriam who scrambled away from the bugs, though she had to know they were meant to be food.

At the quarter hour, I traveled back to the daleth. Phillipa was already there waiting.

"Anything?" I asked, pretending to search the horizon as an excuse to avoid meeting her eyes.

"No." Out of the corner of my eye, she crossed her arms, hugging herself. "What's going on? What happened?"

I sighed. There was no getting around what I had to do... but I still hesitated. She at least deserved to know the truth. I decided to tell her a modified version. "Asher made me use my Gifts to create much larger coin," I said slowly. "He used it to buy an enchanted lamp, but after he left, the coin returned to its original form." I spread my hands apart, eyes wide in innocence. "He knew my Gift only works when connected to living things. He *knew* it was wrong."

When I glanced at Phillipa, she was nodding in agreement.

"Anyway, he's in some serious trouble." I finished vaguely. "I'm sure you had a Jinni Guard visit you as well?"

"Yes!" She gasped. "That's what that was about? I thought it was because of the daleth…"

I turned and hugged her.

It was completely out of character for me, but after a moment of shock, she lifted her arms and embraced me back, comforting *me*.

"I'm so sorry," I said, squeezing my eyes shut against real tears this time. "I wish there was another way."

"What do you m—" Phillipa started to pull back, but she was already shifting beneath my hands, too startled to even fight back.

I chose yellow for her lizard form, to match her warm eyes, which now haunted me with that last look.

Slipping her into the jar, I paused at the way Miriam lay lifelessly at the bottom. Were the holes not adequate? Was she suffocating? Panic gripped me. Holding Phillipa in one hand, I nudged Miriam's little body with my finger.

Her layered eyes blinked open. She lunged at my hand.

Tiny little teeth clamped down hard on my finger.

With a shriek, I flung her off inside the jar, tossing Phillipa in with her, and slammed the lid over them.

The bite had startled me more than anything. Despite her attempts to break skin, there was no blood, just a little sensitivity.

It made it easier to pull the cover flap over the bag. With the jar out of sight, I returned to Jinn through the daleth, and once I was confident that no one else was nearby, I traveled home.

Setting the second jar on top of my dresser beside the first, I dropped wearily onto my bed and stared at the four of them.

While Simon scratched at the walls of the jar—communicating with the girls maybe? I had no idea—Asher lay still where he'd been since this afternoon. It worried me. He needed food and water.

I started with the first, since I'd brought home the crickets in the other jar. To Miriam, I pointed a stern finger and said, "Try a stunt like that again, and I'll turn you into a fly for them to eat. Is that clear?"

Her tiny tongue flicked at me furiously. Eventually, she dipped her head once in what I took to be a nod.

To be safe, I didn't remove the lid, but instead shifted the holes so my hand fit through, scooping up two of the crickets and pulling them out, letting the lid shift back into place.

In the same way, I dropped the crickets into the jar with Simon and Asher. Both of them turned their noses up at the offer.

"You'd better eat," I said, eyeing Asher especially. "I'll be back with water."

My father's drinks came in big glass bottles, and the curved lids would make perfect water dishes. I filled them quickly and added one to each jar.

Once that was done, I sat on the bed again, and we all stared at each other while the crickets hopped around, blissfully unaware.

"Eat," I said again, when none of them moved. "I'm not letting you out, so you might as well get used to it."

They ignored me.

All afternoon, we waited, though they didn't know what I was waiting for.

Finally, the knock came.

Picking up my mirror one last time, I made sure the tears were ready, then strode to the door and opened it.

The same Jinni Guard, Eliezer, stood on the other side. Like the last time, he began by asking if my father was home.

Shaking my head, I summoned up the tears,

letting them fill my eyes and threaten to spill over. "No, but... I have to tell you something." I turned away, leaving the door open for the guard to follow, starting to pace. "I didn't want to say anything before, because I don't want my friends to get in trouble..."

When I trailed off, Eliezer finally stepped into the room, impatient. "Speak the truth. The guard will reward you for your honesty."

I stopped my pacing in the kitchen to dab at my eyes with a towel. Turning to him, I pulled my lips into my mouth, then blurted out. "I think they went to the human world."

His carefully blank expression altered, showing shock before he managed to hide it. "And what makes you think this is the case?"

Choosing my exact words with care, I said, "Asher found a daleth that no one knew about... He showed the rest of us. He wanted us to go through and visit the human world." I then named each of my friends specifically and waited for him to write their names down. This was exactly what needed to happen. Now for the last half-truth. "I didn't want to go."

As soon as I said this, I loosed the tears, letting

them gush down my face, dropping into a chair at the table and putting my head in my hands. "I should've told you, I'm sorry."

"So they went through without you, and they never came back," Eliezer finished for me, wanting to end the story quickly and get away from my tears, just as I'd hoped he would. He shook his head at my friends' foolishness, making notes. "He must have been warned after he stole that lamp," he muttered. To me, he added louder, "Where is this portal located? Do you think these friends you describe know about his theft?"

"I don't know." I sniffed. "Maybe." I gave him my best description of how to find the daleth, slowing the tears, but not cutting them off completely quite yet. I added a red rim to my eyes for good measure.

"Thank you," he said, standing and tucking his notes in a pocket beneath his armor. "I'll be in touch. Most likely the royal family will request your assistance in leading them to the exact location of the daleth."

I nodded, though he was already striding toward the door to leave. "I'm at their service, of course," I whispered, as the door shut on his heels.

Sagging back against the chair, I dried the tears

and drew a deep breath. This nightmare was almost over.

CHAPTER 9

WHEN THE KING AND queen of Jinn summoned me to the castle that same day, I was so relieved that my father was still at work and wouldn't learn of it that I forgot to be nervous until we reached the woven white gate. Very few Jinn besides the guard and those in the upper circles ever had the opportunity to visit the castle. A small flicker of excitement made me pick up my step as we walked down the red-carpeted halls.

Now *this* was luxury and power.

I bet the royal family never has to worry about someone using them or their power. Or if anyone tried, they'd regret it.

When we strode into a grand receiving room, the chandeliers and elaborate décor was dwarfed by the presence of Queen Samaria seated in the center. I recognized her immediately—both her, her husband, and her son all had their own coins in circulation with their faces stamped on them.

Clamping my jaw shut to avoid embarrassing myself, I bowed low. "Your majesty," I murmured, meeting her pearly white eyes rimmed in deep blue. Her pale Jinni skin was more translucent than most, and she was smaller and more frail than I'd expected.

King Jubal strode into the room from the opposite door, equally recognizable, even if he hadn't been wearing the enchanted crown that enhanced all his natural Gifts. His very presence demanded control—of everyone and everything around him. It was the exact opposite of my life. I'd never cared much for the details of royal family, outside of a curiosity about the prince who was so near my own age, but a sudden jealousy gripped me.

The king bent to kiss his wife on the cheek and exchanged a smile with her before he noticed me standing there with the guard. "This is the girl who found the daleth, then?" he asked, shuffling through the papers on his desk. His hair was cut short and he had a neat black beard to match. His energy level was the exact opposite of his wife.

"Yes, your majesty," I answered, wanting to come across strong and believable. "I can take you to it whenever you need." Hopefully right now. The sooner they sealed it off, the better.

"Unfortunately, I don't have a lot of time," the king muttered to his papers, looking up at us finally, eyes glancing over me, then focusing on the guard. "I've asked my son to take over this particular daleth. It will be good practice for him before he becomes king."

My heart beat a little faster. Was I about to meet the prince of Jinn? From the few glimpses I'd had of Prince Shem, I knew he was incredibly handsome, but I'd never met him in person.

The king was still talking, though with his focus on his desk, I couldn't tell if he was speaking to me or the guard. "From my understanding, the portal is in a remote location and only a few of our own were lost to it, before it was reported."

"That's correct, your majesty," the guard replied.

Nodding to himself, the king stroked his beard for a moment. "I'd say it shouldn't require more than a small guard to keep more from going through."

Turning to his wife, he added, "It's those poor children I'm concerned about. The parents will have to be notified. Shem will have to set aside at least one guard at all times to make sure none of them try to go in after their children."

"Shem can handle it," Queen Samaria said soothingly as she joined him at the desk, placing a hand on his arm. She smiled and added, "You know he's been itching for a chance to get away from the castle."

"Yes, well, this might be more than he bargained for," the king grumbled. "It all depends on if they can find a recent use of traveling. Each hour makes it more unlikely, and they've already been gone for at least three or four.

Longer, I thought to myself, but didn't say anything.

"You may go," King Jubal said without looking at us. "The guard will give you your reward for reporting the daleth." As he said this, the guard pressed a small coin purse into my head, turning me by the elbow at the same time.

"Wait." I pulled away, clearing my throat. I couldn't go home without knowing if the portal was closed or not. "Could I please speak to the prince?

I'm worried that he'll have trouble finding the daleth..."

King Jubal nodded in agreement, already turning his back as he waved us out.

The Jinni Guard bowed, leading me from the room while I pondered this new development. I'd been certain they'd seal it immediately. An open portal was dangerous, after all—a human could just as easily stumble on it from their side and enter Jinn. Not to mention young Jinn like us could find it like Asher had and cause enormous amounts of trouble. Only a set number of daleths in strategic locations were usually left open.

"Wait here," the guard said, leaving me in another room decorated with a silver theme, not bothering to bow or say anything else before shutting the door behind him.

Twisting my fingers together, I tried to reassure myself that all of our trails were far too old to be discovered. There'd be no trace of us at this point. If they thought to quickly find some young Jinn making trouble in the human town and return them to their parents by nightfall, they'd be sorely disappointed.

I remembered the coin purse in my hand and opened it. It held enough to buy two enchanted lamps, nearly three! I tucked it into my pocket to consider later.

While I waited, I explored the details of the room, which, although smaller, was as lovely as the previous. The windows stretched from the floor to the ceiling, which was twice my height, and all five of them were framed with silver curtains. The furniture was soft enough to sink into, making me groan with pleasure as I sat down and leaned into it. I could happily stay here forever.

The thought put a dampener on my day, reminding me of the two little jars back home, not to mention my father, who was due for another one of his episodes any day now. *Could* I find a way to stay here? I sighed at the wishful thinking and closed my eyes.

A gentle hand on my shoulder startled me awake. I lurched upright and almost knocked heads with the young Jinn who'd roused me. Blushing fiercely, I apologized and lowered my gaze as I stood, barely allowing myself a glimpse of him. Long black hair tied back, strong cheekbones, and nearly white-eyes like his mother's with a pale blue tint, the young Jinni prince was every bit as handsome as the likenesses I'd seen. He wore a simple woven crown of white-gold on his head. And he had a dimple in one cheek when he smiled.

Bowing low, I said again, "My apologies, Prince Shem."

He laughed lightly. "I hesitated to wake you. Perhaps we should start off our daleth hunt with a nap?"

At first, I thought he was mocking me, but his smile was genuine and open. When I only stood there, lips parted, staring at him, he smiled wider. "I'm only kidding. What's your name, if you don't mind my asking?"

"Bel," I said, then corrected myself. "Jezebel, actually."

He bowed, which was completely unnecessary for the prince of all of Jinn to do, and had me blushing all over again. "A pleasure to meet you, Jezebel." Lifting his elbow out to me, he added, "Would you accompany me on a countryside walk to this daleth of yours? I'd love to take a closer look at it."

My mouth twitched in a small smile, and I took his arm. As I did, the tiniest beginnings of a new plan began to form.

* * *

What I did not expect was for him to lead me *through*

the daleth once we arrived.

"Spread out," he told the four Jinni Guard members—one of whom was Eliezer. They'd followed us through, wearing their full armor, while the prince wore just a breastplate—a silver and gem studded breastplate, more decorative than useful. "See if you can track down any evidence or a trail."

I waited until the guards obeyed before I cleared my throat and asked, "Do you think they'll find anything?" My arm still rested in his, and I couldn't tell if my racing heartbeat was from that or the small chance that these Jinn might still be able to sense that I'd been here too. My entire story would be ruined.

He turned those incredibly pale blue eyes on me, the color of the sky on a cloudless day, quirking one side of his mouth up at my question. Still, he humored me. "They'll be using their Gifts to sift through the human town and the surrounding area without raising any suspicions, to see if there has been any unusual activity."

"Like stupid Simon traveling in broad daylight?" I muttered. At the prince's glance, I added, "That's exactly something he would do." And for good measure, I scrunched up my forehead in concern, staring out toward the town which was visible over the hill. "I hope they find something."

"Don't worry," Prince Shem patted my hand, probably trying to be comforting. "I won't let them leave a human unturned. We'll continue the search, both here, as well as in Jinn, until all possibilities have been exhausted. Though I doubt it will take that long. Their parents will be notified within the hour, but my hope is that we'll deliver their children back to them by the end of the day."

I tried to smile through my frustration, pulling away. I shaded my eyes from the sun, hiding the emotions that must be flickering across my face. At some point, I should see if my Gift would allow me to hide that too. "I've never been in the human world before." Since the guards were gone, I lied through my teeth. "Is it dangerous?"

"Not at all," he said, voice lifting in excitement as he smiled one of his charming, dimpled smiles. He held out his hand again. "How about I show you some of the sights in the human world, since we're already here?" Like his father had said, he was itching to explore.

For the briefest moment, I forgot my anxiety. "What kind of sights?"

"Nothing as beautiful as back home, obviously." He waved his free hand, still holding the other out to me. "But they have creatures you've never heard of before, mountains that rise almost to Jinn, and if that isn't enough to entice you, I could always take you to see the ocean."

I gasped. "We wouldn't go *in* the ocean, would we?"

"Maybe just a toe?" he teased, but I could see that he wasn't serious. "Mother and father would kill me. The truce with the Mere has been in place since my grandmother's reign. Don't worry, I'm not about to risk that." He wiggled the fingers of his outstretched hand playfully.

This prince wasn't half as high and mighty as Asher and the others could be sometimes! I grinned and took his hand.

* * *

That day's search ended as I'd known it would from the start: in failure.

Which was an enormous relief, because I hadn't had a back up plan. Muscles aching from being tensed all day, I dragged myself back through the daleth. This day was almost over.

"You're welcome to come back and check on our progress tomorrow," Prince Shem said as we returned to Jinn, though his brow was furrowed and he wasn't nearly as attentive as he'd been earlier in the day. "I'm sure this is just a hiccup. We'll have better results in the morning."

"I'll see you then," I promised, picking up the seeds of the plan that I'd begun to form earlier. Walking home, I thought through the possibilities. Whatever happened, I'd be a fool to pass up the chance to spend time with the prince. His attention could bring me into new circumstances. As always, this made me think of escaping my father. The sooner, the better. I would keep my eyes open for any opportunities, big or small. And I would keep the reward money to myself. Once home, I hid it in the back of my dresser drawer.

The next day, I traveled to the portal the instant my father left for work, as the sun was still coming up. My friends' parents were already waiting outside the portal when I arrived, speaking with the guard stationed there. They greeted me, but were distracted by the prince and the rest of his guard arriving.

"Jezebel," Prince Shem greeted me warmly, before turning to the parents to reassure them. "There's no need to worry. We have this under control. The guard has handled similar instances in the past, and I've no doubt we'll return your loved ones to you soon."

I noticed he didn't say *by the end of the day* this time.

"Please, if you have work or other duties, feel free to attend to those. You'll be sent word the moment they're found."

Phillipa's father vanished before the prince finished speaking, followed quickly by Asher and Simon's parents. Miriam's mother spoke with the prince a bit longer, but after he continued to soothe her, she left as well, leaving me behind.

"Let's make today count," the prince said to the guards, as he waved them through the daleth.

I bit my lip, thinking he'd forgotten I was there, but then he glanced over his shoulder with a mischievous grin. "Aren't you coming?"

We traveled all across the human world over the next three weeks. My goal quickly became winning him over—as a friend at the very least. A friend in the highest of possible places. One who brought a smile to face and opportunities to my door, instead of trouble and heartache. That was enough for now.

He laughed at me when I encountered my first camel—which tried to spit at me—caught me before I accidentally stepped on my first poisonous snake, and admired me as we soaked up my first human sunset from a mountaintop together.

Just us.

If I didn't know better, I might've said Prince Shem felt as trapped back in Jinn as I did. In fact, a small part of me wondered if I might have a chance as a contender for his heart. Whenever I thought this, though, I'd sigh. There had to be many Jinni girls far richer than I who'd had their sights set on the prince for far longer. What were the chances he'd be interested in someone like me?

I might be a fool to even hope. But those little seeds of a plan began to twist in a new, romantic direction.

As long as I showed up before him and his guards every morning, and stayed after the worried parents left, he always invited me to join him. Whether that meant anything to him or not, *that* was a generous opportunity I wouldn't pass up!

After the first few days, I'd known I'd be gone frequently and would have to somehow break the news to my father.

That same night, I'd fed and watered my little lizard friends, before tucking them underneath my bed out of sight.

Then, I'd waited.

When the doorknob finally turned, signaling my father's arrival home, I was past the point of trembling or twisting my hands anxiously, and in a state of numb exhaustion instead.

"What do you want?" he grunted, slamming the door behind him, and moving to the kitchen.

I trailed behind, clearing my throat. Better to keep it simple. "The Jinni Guard took me on for a short-term assignment. A few weeks at least. I won't be home much, but it's a paid position…" It wasn't a total lie. I thought of the coins hidden in my drawer.

"Fine," my father interrupted. "Maybe you'll be worth something after all. Make sure you bring home every shekel."

It was harder than usual to keep my face calm.

My mother had always been right: People used you. Better to use them first.

* * *

One thing I knew for sure, as I started to fall for the prince and determined to win him over: he would *never* learn my secrets.

But, surprisingly, I was learning his.

"You're nothing like the Jinn at court," he said one day, laughing at my stories of the crowded acropolis.

My face must've fallen, because he was quick to add, "That's a *good* thing, trust me. They're all completely vapid. Conversation always turns to the crown, and if I'd ever consider sharing it with someone."

"Hmm," I drag out the word playfully, stepping closer to him, pretending sudden interest. "And would you?"

When he rolls his eyes, I wink at him the way he's always winking at me, and laugh. "You can't blame them for wondering. After all, have you looked in a mirror lately?"

It was easy to laugh with him, even if I was blushing because I meant it.

And maybe I was being hopeful, but as the weeks passed, part of me thought that maybe when all of this daleth business was over, he might still want to see me?

I made sure to show up at the daleth as early as possible and stay as late as they allowed each day, to make the most of this time. Prince Shem made me feel safe, for the first time in… as long as I could remember. I knew they couldn't search forever, but I didn't want it to end.

Still, it was only a matter of time.

"Tomorrow is likely to be our last day," Prince Shem was saying now as we strolled through a rainforest, stopping to admire a colorful bird with a beak the same size as its body. His voice was low, eyes downcast, as he added, "This isn't the first time we've been unsuccessful in finding missing Jinn, but it doesn't make it any easier."

He offered me a helping hand to step over a fallen log, and after, I was pleased when he continued to hold onto it. I cleared my throat, trying to sound sad as well, when I asked, "Will you tell the parents in the morning?"

"No," he said, taking a deep breath and blowing it out. "We'll set up something formal, at the castle. I probably shouldn't have told you, either, truthfully. But I thought you should know."

"I appreciate that," I said softly, smiling at him. "I'd always prefer to know." My words held multiple meanings, as I gazed up at him.

"Oh, yes?" He grinned at me. "And does that apply to everything? I suppose I should also let you know that you look very lovely today."

"Thank you." I smiled at him. I'd taken to shifting my face the slightest bit to add color to my cheeks and lips, and depth to my lashes and eyes. It could easily be mistaken for makeup and over time I hoped those who knew me would forget I'd ever looked any different. The thought reminded me of my friends, still in lizard form, back at the acropolis.

Prince Shem read my change in expression and misunderstood. "I really shouldn't have told you about tomorrow. You don't have to come if seeing them seal the daleth will be too difficult for you."

I turned away, lifting my hand to my eyes as if to brush away a tear, though in reality I had to hide my anticipation.

Thinking that it might also be my last day with Shem sobered me enough to make my face more mournful. "There's still a small chance they could be found," I said finally. "I'd like to be there, if that's okay. I'll stay out of the way."

He smiled down at me, standing closer than normal. "I'd enjoy that very much."

CHAPTER 10

THOUGH I BROUGHT MY bag along the next day, with the glass jar that held all my lizard friends hidden inside, Prince Shem would not leave my side long enough for me to do anything with it. "I don't want you to face this alone," he said softly at the start of the day, tucking a stray piece of my hair behind my ear.

It was exactly what I'd wanted from him, at the worst possible time.

Outwardly, I'd smiled and leaned into his hand.

Inwardly, the tension in my shoulder blades and neck grew painful enough to cause a splitting headache. As the day passed, we ate food from the castle and waited.

When Shem asked why I'd brought the bag, I said, "It's for good luck, I guess—" slipping my hand inside without opening the flap, I pulled out one of my gold armbands that I'd included for this exact reason "—just some of their things in case we find them today."

That was enough to set him at ease and keep him from asking more. But it wasn't enough to distract him from his mission. Shem fastened himself to my side, determined to be there when I broke down.

Though I considered faking it, I brushed that aside at first. By the end of the day though, I could hardly think, much less answer Shem's persistent questions. Fortunately, he interpreted that as anxiety over my lost friends.

Still, when Eliezer gave his evening report to Shem, I asked them for one more hour. "Please," I begged, leaning into the prince's arm and pressing a hand to my face where I'd summoned a sheen of tears. "A little bit longer. Just in case?"

Prince Shem was quick to agree.

I waited until he'd sent the guards out again

before I pretended to gasp and whirled to face him. "Have they checked the human towns thoroughly? Because Asher was bragging about trying to take a human captive. He was so hungry for power. But…" I shrugged delicately. "Well, you know, he's basically Giftless. Do you think there could be a chance the awful humans took him hostage instead?"

"It's doubtful," Prince Shem said, pursing his lips, though his eyes strayed to the town. "They've done quite a few searches in that vicinity already without disturbing the human life in the area. I hate to disappoint you…"

"I understand." I rubbed his arm, lowering my gaze. "Would you consider asking Eliezer to check, for my sake? Please?"

Once again, the prince was as moldable as if I'd shape-shifted him myself. "Of course. That's the least I can do. I'll catch up with Eliezer and ask. Be back in a moment."

The instant he left, I strode a dozen paces to make tracking me more difficult, and traveled to the farthest place I could think of: the rainforest we'd explored the day before.

Kneeling next to a moss-covered fallen tree, I opened my bag and pulled out the jar, lifting the lid and pouring out the lizards inside onto the wide log.

Asher and Simon blended into the moss easily, and with a simple touch, I muted the vibrant pinks, oranges, and yellows of Miriam and Phillipa to allow them to blend into the greenery as well.

"That should help you hide from any predators," I said to them softly, though there was absolutely no one else listening. I didn't need to understand them to know what they were thinking. "I wish I could return you to your true forms."

The wrinkles on my brow were real for once, and I had to look away at the foliage around us as I struggled with my guilt. "It's just not possible. You would find your way back and turn me in, and I can't risk it. I hope some day you'll understand that you did this to yourselves when you tried to use me for your own gain."

I turned to the fifth lizard.

The one I'd added last night.

When my father had come home, I'd already talked myself into it and out of it multiple times. But as he'd stepped inside he'd started in on the same subject as every other night that week. "Have you been paid yet?"

I didn't answer, but this time he didn't wait for one either.

"No, you haven't," he snarled. "Because you're a filthy little liar. I checked with the Jinni Guard today. You're not working for them, and you never were."

This made my decision that much easier. The only part that made me nervous was touching him. I couldn't remember a kind touch from him in years.

"Fetch me a drink!" He yelled as he flung the door shut with a bang, moving toward his favorite chair and dropping into it. "That's all you're good for. It's about time you get a real job and support your father in his old age after I've supported you all these years."

I bided my time, enduring his ranting as I quietly approached.

Seated in his chair, disregarding me, he never had any warning.

"I expect you to come home with real coin by the end of the week or—" He took the drink, still speaking, but cut off startled when I gripped his wrist.

By the time he let go of the bottle to stop me, he was too late. The glass shattered on the floor, spraying dark liquid across the carpet and my legs.

I ignored it.

He was the fifth lizard that I'd added to the jar, and that I'd carried with me throughout the day up until this moment.

I stared down at him now where he crouched, stiff and frozen, apart from the others, tongue flicking wildly, probably trying to scream at me.

He didn't blend into the foliage like my former friends; I stared down at him considering.

In the end, I left his coloring vibrant red.

Though I'd barely been gone more than five minutes, I returned to find Prince Shem pacing. His hair stood at odd ends, as if he'd run his hands through it multiple times. "Where were you?" he called, running toward me, taking my hands and touching my face, as if to check for some harm that could've happened in that short time.

I reached into my bag, pulling out a large pink flower that faded into a soft orange center. Licking my lips, I held it up to show him. "I just wanted a little keepsake of our time here," I whispered huskily, dipping my head to look up at him through my lashes. "I should've told you, but I worried you'd think it was silly."

He touched the soft petal of the flower, smiling easily. "I don't think that's silly at all."

"Good," I said, reaching into my bag again to

pull out a second flower. "Because I got one for you too." I didn't have to fake the blush on my cheeks for him.

The Jinni Guard returned one by one, pretending not to see the way their prince stared at the lowly Jinni girl. Once we were all there, we returned to Jinn through the portal, and the guard began the slow process of sealing it shut.

Permanently.

The others would never be able to get home. Never be able to take advantage of me again, or tell anyone my true Gift.

A small pang of guilt reminded me there was also no taking it back. No changing my mind.

Once the portal was sealed, that was it.

"I'm so sorry we didn't find your friends," Prince Shem said, offering me his arm as he often did, not to lead me anywhere this time, but simply for comfort.

I blinked back real tears, though I probably could've let them fall. Clearing my throat, I said softly, "And *I'm* sorry they ever found that awful daleth in the first place."

I meant it. I would miss them.

Taking my first deep breath in weeks, I

wondered why I didn't feel much better. No one was hounding me anymore. If I had anything to say about it, no one would control me ever again. Clutching the prince's arm tighter, I sighed. It was unexpectedly lonely.

The space between the trees began to glow white, growing brighter until I had to squint. As the guards chanted their spell too quietly for us to hear where we stood, the glow outlined the invisible portal and made it's full size and scope clear. Eyes stinging, I was about to look away when the glow snapped together and disappeared in the span of a breath.

All at once, the trees on each side seemed lifeless and dull. We waited anxiously as the first guard stepped through the space, followed by the others, testing every speck of the former portal to be certain it was gone. No one disappeared.

All four members of the Jinni Guard stepped back as one, signaling that they were finished sealing the portal.

This might be the last time I would see Prince Shem.

On a whim, I sucked in a deep breath and asked in a rush. "Is there any chance you have other portals you need help sealing? Or… searching for…?" I trailed off, realizing I hadn't actually done either of those things. Technically, my presence had been completely unnecessary after day one.

"Now that you mention it, I believe there might be." He winked at me, squeezing my fingers in a way that gave me little flutters of excitement in my belly. "Perhaps I can call on you and your father soon with a new mission?"

I let my face fall.

"What is it?" he asked, turning me by the shoulders to face him and tilting my chin up until I met his eyes. "What's wrong?"

Once more, I called up tears, letting them hover right on the edge of overflowing. I'd gotten quite practiced at this particular skill. "My father is gone. He left me and made it clear he wasn't coming back."

Prince Shem frowned in confusion. Not many Jinni fathers would consider abandoning their children. However, if he'd asked around about me at all in our last few weeks together, or even if he sent his guards to inquire now, it wouldn't take much searching to discover that's exactly the kind of father I had.

A vision of a bright red lizard on a mossy log flashed across my eyes, but I blinked it away.

I gave the prince a sad smile. "I'm all alone now. And I may not have my home for much longer. But you may still call anytime. As long as I'm there, I'm at your service."

"Leave us," Prince Shem waved at the guards in response, not breaking my gaze.

They didn't *actually* leave, but they did travel a good fifty paces away to keep watch over their prince from a distance instead, giving him the privacy he'd requested.

To me, the prince said more gently. "I can't imagine you being forced to live on your own." He lifted my hand, placing it over his heart. "You must come to the castle. We have more than enough room. I couldn't bear for you to be hurt when you could easily find a place with us."

It was more than I'd dared to hope for. "Are you certain?"

"Very." He grinned.

"I don't deserve your kindness," I said, taking a deep breath, as my future opened up before me with thousands of possibilities.

I would do whatever it took to make this dream permanent. To never, ever suffer the manipulation of others again.

I brought his hand to my mouth and pressed my

lips to his skin, giving him a rare, true smile, as I added, "But I humbly accept."

THE END.

...

If you loved this book, support the author by leaving a review—it helps more than you know!

WANT MORE OF JEZEBEL'S STORY?

There's a century that passes between this story and The Stolen Kingdom series. Sign up for my author newsletter and let me know if you'd enjoy seeing another installment of Jezebel's story in the future.

Once part of my newsletter you'll be the first to learn about new releases, plus receive exclusive content for both readers and writers!

WWW.BETHANYATAZADEH.COM/CONTACT

READ THE STOLEN KINGDOM SERIES NEXT ...

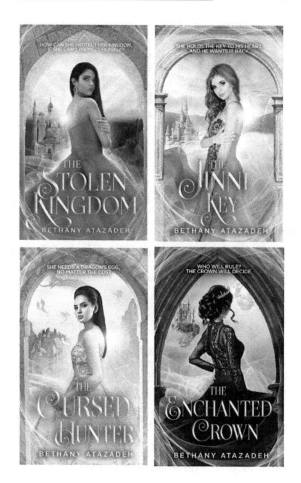

PLUS a bonus scene from Gideon in my newsletter.

THE
STOLEN
KINGDOM

A dainty princess and a friendly genie are replaced with a tough heroine who fights back and a magical race everyone fears in this addicting fairy tale twist on Aladdin.

Princess Arie never expects to manifest a forbidden Jinni's Gift. When she begins to hear the thoughts of those around her, she hides it to the best of her ability.

But to her dismay, the Gift is growing out of control. When a neighboring king tries to force her hand in marriage and steal her kingdom, discovery becomes imminent. Just one slip could cost her throne. And her life.

A lamp, a heist, and a Jinni hunter's crew of thieves are her only hope for removing this Gift—

and she must remove it before she's exposed. Or die trying.

The Stolen Kingdom is a loose "Aladdin" retelling. Set in a world that humans share with Mermaids, Dragons, and the elusive Jinni, this isn't the fairytale you remember...

AVAILABLE NOW

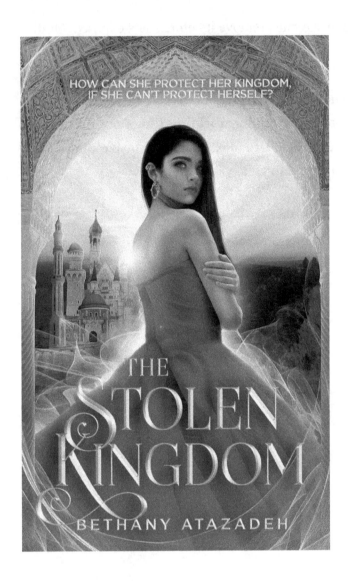

HOW CAN SHE PROTECT HER KINGDOM,
IF SHE CAN'T PROTECT HERSELF?

THE STOLEN KINGDOM

BETHANY ATAZADEH

READ THE FIRST CHAPTER...

Chapter 1

Arie

MY HANDS SAT CLENCHED in my lap. I didn't play with the gold and pearl fabric of my dress, or tap my fingers on my throne, or even twitch an eyebrow. But underneath my skirts, my toes tapped a steady rhythm, counting down the seconds until dinner.

Normally, I adored holding court with my father. Learning to rule meant everything to me.

But not today.

Not for the last few months, actually.

We'd listened to the nobles list their complaints

for nearly four hours now. My head buzzed with voices, like a swarm of locusts. The more people in the room, the louder they pulsed until the pressure was unbearable.

At least if I kept still and avoided drawing attention to myself, it was more manageable. I sat as quiet as the serving girl concealed in the corner. But she wasn't wearing the gold circlet of a princess woven through delicately braided hair. She didn't have long, black curls falling on expensive gold-lace sleeves. Or a white pearl dress, designed to remind eligible men of a wedding gown. Lucky girl.

A white-haired Shah, lord of a small province in our kingdom, stood in the open space before my father and I.

"King Mahdi," Shirvan-Shah railed, in the middle of an outburst. "I didn't want to bring this to your attention if I didn't have to, but this dispute is over far more than my son and Marzban-Shah's daughter." Spittle flew from his mouth as he paced the marble floor between us and his rapt audience, who waited their turn. "It pains me to speak of such things, but I'm afraid I must..." He dropped to his knees before my father's throne and bowed his head.

I wanted to roll my eyes.

"As I'm sure you're aware, the Marzban family

has Jinni-blood running through their veins…"

I leaned forward.

Too late, I caught myself and sat back.

No one noticed. All eyes were glued to Shirvan-Shah, who let the silence draw out, until it lay thick and expectant over the room. He cleared his throat and stage whispered, "I believe she may have a Jinni's Gift."

Horrified gasps and murmurs replaced the silence. The corners of his mouth twitched upward as he stood. I found myself hating him.

"That's a strong accusation to make without proof," my voice rang out. I couldn't help myself. "What if she's innocent?" I clutched the arms of my throne, leaning forward. "Are you willing to risk ruining a young girl's life simply because she didn't find your son a good match?"

Every onlooker shifted their gaze from Shirvan-Shah to me. The hum in the room grew louder. I regretted my words immediately.

"Arie," my father scolded. It wasn't my place to judge in these hearings. Not yet. My role was to learn and observe.

"Sorry, Baba." I bowed my head, hating the disappointment in his tone.

Whispers grew louder as I became the center of

attention. My head throbbed.

"Continue, Shah." My father tipped his gold scepter toward Shirvan-Shah.

As the focus shifted back to the older man, I sighed softly, resisting the urge to sag back against my throne. Imitating the serving girl once more, I sat stiff and upright, barely breathing.

The Shah eyed me before easing back into his speech. "The princess makes a fair point." He dipped his head toward me, tenting his bony fingers. "However, I fear Marzban-Shah's daughter's Gift is evident. There's rumor of her sheets turning to iron, as well as her bathtub, and other common household items."

This time I guarded against any reaction. When those around me gasped, I chastised myself, *Don't be too still either.*

"What kind of Gifting is this?" my father muttered.

"I'd never heard of its likeness, Your Highness," Shirvan-Shah stepped closer, though he didn't lower his voice in the slightest. "There are too many different Jinni's Gifts to keep track of. I thought perhaps it was like Aaran-Shah's Gift, where he knows what to plant and helps the seedlings grow. Or Yazdan-Shah's son who can turn commonplace items into gold. But it seems that, as usual, this woman's Gift is dangerous."

Why do they see danger in women while men are trusted? I pushed down the urge to question him, but it was difficult. *Her Gift seems harmless.* Especially when compared to other Jinni's Gifts I'd heard of growing up—the ability to travel across kingdoms in a heartbeat, shape-shifting, swimming in the depths with the Mere-folk, soul-stealing… That last one may have been more of a child's bedtime story than truth, but I'd never been entirely certain. *How can we know anything about the Jinn when even the entrance to their land is a secret?*

"Thank you for bringing it to my attention," my father said with a sigh. The laws regarding Gifted women had been passed before I was born. While the stories differed on how the decision came to be, the verdict was clear: Gifted women were dangerous. They must go to trial and be closely examined. If they failed the trial, their Gift was to be severed.

I'd been too young to witness the last Severance, but my blood ran cold as my father added, "She will be dealt with immediately."

Dealt with.

I clenched my teeth to keep a flood of words from escaping.

A neighboring prince's Gift had surfaced just two months ago. Of course, his Gift had been deemed safe. But it'd been years since anyone had discovered a Gifted woman.

My father turned to the cleric. "Schedule a hearing. And arrange a search party to see if anyone can find a Jinni. We'll likely need a Severance." The cleric scratched notes on his parchment.

The blood drained from my face. The hum in the room grew louder. Another Shah stood to go next, but I stopped listening. My heart pounded as I waited for the worst of it to manifest. Bracing myself, I was still completely unprepared when it happened.

The princess looks like she's about to faint.

It was someone else's thought forming in my mind—the tone of it high and shrill. Though I'd doubted the sensation when the episodes had first begun, certain I was losing my mind, it was undoubtedly a thought. Now, I could usually distinguish which thoughts belonged to me versus those around me.

I tried to ignore the stranger in my head. But as one of my ladies-in-waiting, Havah, stepped forward to offer me a cup of cool water, her thoughts intruded as well.

She looks horrible.

It took everything in me not to wince as I accepted the cup. As I thought about the ruling, it was hard to swallow.

I didn't know the full details of a Severance. But the Gifted woman's fate was certain: death.

Whether a day, a week, or even a month or two after the fact, she wouldn't live long. They always said it was an accident. The women hung themselves, or slipped in the bath, or fell from their horse... But I knew better. Someone killed them. What a horrible punishment for an innocent girl who couldn't help herself. I hated that I had to keep silent. But if I didn't...

If my kingdom—if my own father ever learned of my Jinni's Gift, would he do that to me?

* * *

When the bell tolled in the keep across the castle, my father dismissed everyone to get ready for dinner. "We'll resume with Yik-Shah in two day's time."

I stood a split second after he did, rushing toward the back door to avoid the crowds as I all but fled the throne room, trailed by my ladies-in-waiting. I led the way up the curving staircase, down a long hallway, and entered my rooms.

My sitting room at the entrance held a dozen comfortable chairs and a table, meant for entertaining guests without allowing them the intimacy of my bedroom, though there was a small bed hidden along the wall where my ladies-in-waiting took turns staying the night in case I required anything.

"I'll call if I have need." I dismissed them, entering my personal rooms. Locking the door, I crossed to my bathing room and stared into the floor length mirror.

Havah was right. My warm, golden skin was pale; a sharp contrast to the soft black hair that flowed loosely over my shoulders. I touched my lips, still a vivid red, and the paint came away. Dipping a clean towel in fresh water, I scrubbed until my face was clean. Water dripped on my elegant dress, but I didn't care. As I set down the towel, my hand shook.

A knock sounded.

With a sigh, I moved to open the door. "Time to get you ready for dinner, Arie-zada," Havah called me by my childhood nickname, a shortened version of my formal title, *Shazada*. She stepped through the door, to stand beside it. *You go through so many dresses.*

I turned to hide my reaction as I waved her in, moving to the balcony for some fresh air.

"Sirjan-Shah paid you so many compliments during the last courtship tour, I could hardly keep up," Havah said.

I stared at the sea, eyes searching for a glimpse of one of the Mere out of years of habit, though I'd yet to see one. Waves crashed against the cliffs below, and I struggled to tune out Havah's thoughts as I replied, "His compliments were shallow." I knew, because his flattery was interlaced with thoughts of my treasure and how he could best get his hands on it.

Or maybe you're shallow, Havah's thoughts washed over me like a bitter rain.

I winced.

She ignores them all. I couldn't tune her out, no matter how hard I tried. *I'd give anything for attention like that.*

When I glanced back to where she sifted through my closet for a suitable evening style, she only smiled. If not for the way my Gift had manifested over the last six months, I'd never have guessed her thoughts.

What did she have to be jealous of? Her bronze skin was smoother than mine, her lips fuller. Her brown eyes more slanted and her hand more talented at lining them with coal. Her hair shone just as dark and long as my own. We could be sisters, but for my tiara and the quality of my clothes.

"What about Tahran-Shah?" she asked, pulling out a red, sleeveless dress that would cling to me. She helped me remove the white pearl gown. "He's very handsome and his—"

"Is there anyone who interests you, Havah?" I interrupted, stepping into the red dress.

"No one, Arie-zada." She used the term of endearment almost like a weapon. Making me like her. Want her by my side. Except now that I knew the truth, I couldn't hear it the same way.

I allowed her to lace the dress tight, so it wouldn't slip, though I secretly drew deep breaths until she finished. No sense in being miserable during dinner.

Havah held out the top piece to finish off my dress. I slipped my arms into the gold lace sleeves. It settled delicately over my collarbone and shoulders, making the ensemble appear modest, though it didn't even reach the dress. Havah buttoned it in the back.

How could any man want a mere servant when they're in your presence?

I swallowed a sigh. The constant invasion of thoughts was exhausting. Even if people weren't thinking of me, there was always an ominous, low hum in my mind. The hum would swell into a buzz and threaten to form. It made me so tired, I could hardly think.

I swayed on my feet.

She wants to be crowned heir apparent on her 18th birthday, yet she can't make it through a full day of court.

"Just stop."

Havah froze.

Hands outstretched, with a hair pin still in her mouth, she met my gaze, confusion written across her face.

Not again. I cursed myself inwardly for yet another slip. I couldn't seem to control my tongue.

"Stop... worrying over the men in my life, my friend." I smiled to take the edge off my words. "I know you want the best for me."

"Ah...yes, Arie-zada. Of course. As you wish..." Only a tiny crease between Havah's brows gave her feelings away as she pinned my thick curls up, to better offset the enormous gold earrings dangling from my ears. As I turned to stand before the mirror, they tickled my shoulders.

Just as I'd begun to relax, Havah returned to her previous train of thought, *How can she rule Hodafez, if she can't even stomach a Severance?*

I ground my teeth. *For the love of Jinn, can't you think about anything else for two seconds?* I wanted to scream the words, but I managed to stay silent for once, until she was done.

So beautiful, she thought, stepping back, and this time the tone was a bit kinder. More admiration, less contempt.

"Thank you," I murmured into the silence.

She paused once more.

My eyes widened. I forced myself to breathe. Lifting my chin, I stared at myself in the mirror, patting my hair. "Ah... it looks lovely."

It was enough.

"You always look lovely," Havah replied, moving to store the leftover hair pins.

I slowly let out my breath.

Each time I slipped up, I feared the worst.

I reached out to grasp Havah's hands, searching her smooth face for a friend, wanting—needing—to know I wasn't alone. "I'm sorry I snapped earlier. It's just... it's impossible to know if a suitor is truly interested in me..."

I stopped, unable to put into words the real problem: I knew exactly what they were interested in. My wealth. My throne. Even my people, occasionally. But never me.

Havah's face softened. Her hands squeezed mine back. "How could anyone not love you? You only need to let your guard down long enough for a nice young man to get to know you. Now come, it's time for dinner."

I let her lead me through the front room where my other ladies stood waiting, out into the carpeted hallway that softened our footsteps, and downstairs toward the dining hall. The hall that held an entire room filled with people eager to prove Havah false and bring my worst nightmares to life.

She was wrong. No one could know me, or the truth. *If they knew the truth, they wouldn't love me. They'd want to kill me.*

AVAILABLE NOW

ACKNOWLEDGMENTS

At this point in publishing, I think it's safe to say I have the best team of creative people possible!

My talented critique partners, Brittany Wang and Jessi Elliott, always catch my blind spots and help me brainstorm ways to fix huge plot holes. There are certain story elements that I'm *terrible* at, and thankfully they always call me out on it and help me figure out how to make it the best it can be!

My trusted group of beta readers, Amelia Nichele, Athena Marie, Emma Woodham, Katherine Schober, and Lia Anderson, also provided a ton of insight into what could make this story better. As always, after I finished implementing their feedback, I wondered how I could've possibly thought the story was done before that!

My cover designer, Mandi Lynn at Stone Ridge Books, knocked it out of the park with this latest design—it's my favorite one yet!

My patrons need a special shout out for their financial support and faith in my work—you all make it possible for me to focus on writing and make me want to give it my all so I don't let you down!

My wonderful mama always agrees to proofread, thanks mom! You're the best!

My sweet husband always supports my career choices and helps me navigate each new stage of the journey. Love you babe!

And finally, to you, my reader—thank you for taking a chance on this story! I hope you enjoyed every moment and I can't wait to hear what you think of it!

GLOSSARY

Asher (ASH-er) – friend of Jezebel's, son of Methuselah, son of Obed

Daleth – Jinni portal into human world (Hebrew word for door)

Eliezer (Ell-ee-AY-zuhr) – Jinni Guard, son of Japeth, son of
    Hezekiah

Jezebel (JEZ-zuh-bell) – young Jinni shape-shifter

Jinn/Jinni (Gin/GIN-nee) – Jinn is the name of the country and the
    race of Jinn as a whole (i.e. *the Jinn, the land of Jinn*); Jinni is
    the singular, used to refer to an individual Jinni and also as a
    possessive (i.e. *a Jinni, a Jinni's Gift*)

Jinni Guard (GIN-nee Guard) –

King Jubal (JOO-bull) – king of Jinn

Lacklore – a beast in Jinn with an ox head and bear body

Lamech – store owner

Master Yeshiva – a Jinni teacher who was banished to the human
    world

Mere (Meer) – meremaids and mereman, also known as mere-folk

Miriam (MEER-ree-uhm) – friend of Jezebel's

Phillipa (PHIL-lip-uh) – friend of Jezebel's

Prince Shem (Sheh-mm) – prince of Jinn

Queen Samaria (Saw-MARE-ree-uh) – queen of Jinn

Resh – capital city of Jinn (Hebrew word for head)

River Mem – the river that runs through the city of Resh

Shekel (Sh-ECK-ell) – a Jinni coin of such little value it's often
    thrown away

Simon (SIGH-muhn) – friend of Jezebel's

Urim (Yer-uhm) – and island in Jinn

Three Unbreakable Laws of Jinn:

1) Never use a Gift to deceive

2) Never use a Gift to steal

3) Never use a Gift to harm another

Bethany Atazadeh is best known for her young adult fantasy novels, The Stolen Kingdom Series, which won the Best YA Author 2020 Minnesota Author Project award. She is obsessed with stories, chocolate, and her corgi puppy, Penny.

Using her degree in English with a creative writing emphasis, Bethany enjoys helping other writers through her YouTube aka "AuthorTube" writing channel (below) and Patreon page (also below).

If you want to know more about when Bethany's next book will come out, visit her website below where you can sign up to receive monthly emails with exciting news, updates, and book releases.

CONNECT WITH BETHANY ON:
Website: www.bethanyatazadeh.com
Instagram: @authorbethanyatazadeh
YouTube: www.youtube.com/bethanyatazadeh
Patreon: www.patreon.com/bethanyatazadeh